16 On the Block

A Babygirl Drama

16 On the Block

A Babygirl Drama

Babygirl Daniels

www.urbanbooks.net

Urban Books
1199 Straight Path   WPK
West Babylon, NY 11704

16 On the Block ©copyright 2009 Urban Books, LLC

ISBN- 13: 978-1-60162-184-9
ISBN- 10: 1-60162-184-1

First Printing February 2009
Printed in the United States of America

10 9 8 7 6 5 4 3 2

Distributed by Kensington Publishing Corp.
Submit Wholesale Orders to:
Kensington Publishing Corp.
C/O Penguin Group (USA) Inc.
Attention: Order Processing
405 Murray Hill Parkway
East Rutherford, NJ 07073-2316
Phone: 1-800-526-0275
Fax: 1-800-227-9604

Chapter One

"Summer"

As we sat in front of the judge I could feel my older sister, Trish, squeezing my hand tightly in anticipation. We held onto each other for dear life as we waited to hear the judge's decision. The fact that this old, wrinkled white man could make or break my future had my stomach in knots. I wondered if he knew that he held my fate in his hands; that if he made the wrong decision he could ruin the rest of my life. Never mind the decision I had made that had landed me here in the first place.

This judge, this man, this stranger, had the power to take away the little bit of hope that I had managed to hold onto from my childhood. I needed him to be on my side. Trish and I needed him to be on *our* side.

He eyed us both suspiciously, pulling his silver, wire-framed glasses down to the bridge of his pointy nose. He had a nose like Ashley Tisdale's, that white chick from *High School Musical*, before she got her nose job, only the judge's was bigger as he looked condescendingly down at us from the high rise chair in which he sat.

I'd rehearsed in the mirror all morning long the facial expression that I was now trying to hold onto my brown, oval face. After practicing a look of desperation and sadness, I had settled on an expression that was a cross between weak and pitiful; although nothing about me was either of those. But I needed this man to feel sorry for me and not see me as some strong-willed girl who could take whatever he dished out.

I stood there, still desperately trying to hold that expression on the outside even though I was heated on the inside. I hated the amount of power that he had over me, that this system had over me, and right at that moment, I decided that no one would ever have that amount of power over me again. How could he judge me? He hadn't seen the things that I'd seen or survived through the situations I'd overcome. He didn't know my struggle or my heartache.

Trish and I never had it easy; we were always what society calls underprivileged children. Ghetto babies from the west side of Detroit, we were expected to fail from the very beginning, and I guess we didn't disappoint. But it wasn't our fault. We were simply dealt a bad hand, and on top of that, the deck we were playing with was a few cards short to begin with.

We were raised by a single mother because Daddy didn't want to take claim to what he called the biggest mistake of his life. When our mother got with him, he was a married man with a wife and kid at home already, so of course he had no room for us. It seems to me that after him being a deadbeat father for my sister's first five years in this world, my mama would have wised up and kicked him to the curb instead of having another baby with him. But then again, if she had, then I would not be here.

After discovering that he had another baby on the way, he ditched us all, the born and the unborn, which left our mom with two girls to raise singlehandedly. So she did what a lot of black mothers do: she took on two, sometimes three jobs to make sure that we never wanted for the necessities. We always had clothes to wear on our backs and shoes for our feet. They may not have been covered in brand names, but we had something that was better than nothing. She made sure that Trish and I never went hungry, although sometimes she didn't get to eat herself. Mama never fixed her plate first, and she always pretended to keep busy by cleaning up the kitchen until she was certain that we'd had enough and didn't want seconds.

"Are you gonna eat, Mama?" Trish and I would often ask her.

"You girls go ahead. I'm not that hungry right now. If I get hungry after I'm finished cleaning up, I might eat something," she'd say without looking up from the dishes in the sink.

She never looked at us when she told us that. Guess she didn't want to lie to our faces. When we got older, we realized that *might* meant she'd eat only if there was any food left over. *Might* wasn't based upon her hunger. Of course she was hungry. She worked two jobs. But hungry or not, she'd go without if need be. Her only concern was that my sister and I go to bed with full bellies. Anything short of that and she felt she'd failed us.

Mama never failed us, though. Our lights were never cut off, our water never ran dry, and our house was always clean. No, we didn't have a lot of money, but we had a great mother and we had each other. That was all we needed. You know what they say, though: a good thing doesn't last forever, and our happiness ended when I was only eight.

Trish would take care of me while our mother worked as a cashier in a convenience store on the weekends. She still always tried not to put too much on Trish. She didn't want Trish to feel like I was her responsibility, so when Trish would ask to spend the night at one of her friends' houses, Mama would automatically say yes, which meant I would have to go to work with her.

DING! DING!

I hear that bell to this day in my dreams. It's a sound that I can never forget.

One day when Mama had to take me to work with her, I was lying behind the counter, drifting into a comfortable sleep when I heard the bell signal that a customer had walked into the store. Mama had already taught me to stay hidden so that she wouldn't lose her job. The last thing she needed was for the customers to start reporting to her boss that she was bringing her little girl to work. But it was either that, leave me at home alone, or leave me out in the car. That is a hard choice that single moms all over the world still have to make on a daily basis.

It wasn't the first time that I had been to her job, so I knew to stay out of sight. I ran into the back storage room and peeked out from around some boxes as I watched the man who had entered the store. Everything was normal for a minute, until I heard the harsh demand of a male voice.

"Give me all the money in the cash register!"

Instinctively, my young body froze in horror. I immediately knew that Mama was in trouble. She grabbed a bag from behind the counter, leaving out the spiel store clerks were trained to ask regarding paper or plastic. She chose plastic out of habit because that's what most people requested.

"Hurry up before I blow your head off!" was his second command, right before his third, "Put all of the money in the bag!"

I cringed at the sound of the voice. I was so afraid that I peed on myself, the warm liquid drenching my legs as I shook involuntarily. I knocked over some empty boxes, causing the intruder to look toward the back room where I was hidden. I quickly dipped back behind the boxes before he could see me, and then just barely peeked with one eye.

"What was that?" the man screamed as he pointed a gun in Mama's face.

"Nothing, probably rats!" she said nervously. Her voice shook, and I could see her eyes searching for me. The man noticed it too and stepped to the back of the store.

"Who is back here?" he yelled.

"No!" my mother screamed as she ran from behind the counter and grabbed the man in her attempt to halt him.

Boom!

It was the loudest thing I'd ever heard. My ears popped instantly and everything in the store sounded muffled as I watched in horror. Mama fell to her knees, and her head hit the floor with a sickening thud.

"Ma!" I screamed as I burst from the back room. My presence seemed to startle the man because he raised his gun to shoot me too. But for some reason, he never pulled the trigger.

"Dang!" he yelled. He grabbed the plastic bag of stolen money and fled as I ran to Mama and fell to my knees in an attempt to save her. I couldn't, though. I was too late. She was dead, and for a long time, I felt like it was my fault. If she had not been trying to protect me, she would still be alive. She'd sacrificed many meals so that I could eat, and now she had sacrificed her entire life so that I could live. Every decision Mama had ever made was selfless. And now here I had to make only one decision, to be still and be quiet, and yet I couldn't even do that. If only I could have been a little bit quieter, if only I had just gone into the back storage room and stayed put without trying to be nosy, Mama would never have been shot and my family would never have been ripped apart. Trish and I would have been raised at home with Mama instead of being forced into a group home.

Fortunately, we were placed together, but being five years older than me, Trish got out first. She only spent five years in the home, while I had been forced to spend ten of the longest years of my life in a place that I dreaded worse than death.

When Trish was released, she promised to come back for me. When she petitioned the court for custody, they told her that she was too young and unstable to care for someone my age. They assured her that on my sixteenth birthday they would reconsider letting me leave with her. Now, here we sat in the courtroom on my sweet sixteen, hoping and praying that the judge would let me go.

Please let him let me go, I thought as my grip on Trish's hand tightened. After reviewing Trish's proof that she had acquired a two-bedroom apartment, one of which was meant for me, and looking over the information about the high school that I would hopefully be attending, the judge sighed heavily and removed his glasses. He massaged his temples and then folded his hands on his big mahogany desk.

"Something inside me is telling me not to do this, but I am going to ignore my better judgment and give you young ladies a chance," he said. "After what happened to your mother, I feel like the two of you were never given a chance to excel. I don't want to keep the two of you apart any longer than necessary.

So, through my authority as a judge in this state of Michigan, I hereby declare you, Trish Flynt, legal guardian over minor, Summer Flynt. I wish you ladies luck, and I hope that we aren't forced to cross paths in the future. Stay out of trouble," the judge instructed sternly.

I couldn't help but to release the tears that came from my eyes. It was like I had let the flood gates up and allowed all of my emotions to flow out of my heart. "Oh my God! Thank you," I cried as I hugged Trish tightly.

"Happy B-day, Summer. I told you I would never leave you in there," Trish stated through her own veil of tears.

We rushed out of the building hand in hand, running like two kids through the hallways until we finally reached daylight. To my surprise, there was a brand new Lincoln Navigator with limousine tint and twenty-four-inch rims sitting curbside, waiting for us.

"Is this your car?" I asked as Trish opened the rear door and motioned for me to get inside.

"Nah, shorty, this me," the male driver responded, surprising me. "I'm Boss."

"Summer," I replied as I hopped into the car, wondering just who he was the boss of.

Trish climbed in and Boss pulled away from the curb, burning rubber as he peeled out. It felt so good to be out of the clutches of the system. Everything around me now looked different. The actual appearance of things hadn't changed; they just seemed more appealing because I was viewing things through free eyes.

Boss cruised through the city streets until he pulled into a set of high rise apartments on the bank of the Detroit River. I got out and admired the luxury building before me. Trish opened up her door and got out behind me.

"You like?" I heard Trish ask over my shoulder.

I nodded. "I feel like Orphan Annie. I think I'm gonna like it here."

"Yo, Trish, I'ma holla at you later," Boss called from inside the car. "I'll give you a couple hours to get your sis settled, but don't have me waiting for too long. You know we have to handle that," Boss stated before driving away.

"My stuff!" I turned around and said to Trish as our ride drove away. "I still need to go get all my stuff."

"New home, new beginnings, so you'll need new stuff. I'll take you shopping. But for now . . ." Trish draped her arms around me and smiled proudly. "Welcome home, sis." She grabbed my hand and led the way inside my new dwelling.

When I saw Trish's apartment I was impressed.

The minute we walked into the door my feet hit a hardwood floor so shiny that I could almost see myself. To my left was the kitchen area that had a half wall that separated it from the living area. The kitchen had black appliances with stainless steel accessories. The dining set was a thick glass table with four chairs that looked more like king's thrones than dinette chairs. They were covered in a silver, satin-like material. The table was set as if food was cooking on the stove and Trish was about to serve up feast—wine glasses with silver cloth napkins tucked inside and all.

The living area was furnished with a rust-colored suede oversized sofa and chair with an ottoman. There was no coffee table sitting in front of the couch like most living areas, but instead, just a rust, orange, and white plush rug. The absence of a coffee table made the room look bigger.

I looked around at all of the nice accessories Trish had decorated the room with. I was still impressed, but I wasn't stupid. I may have been young, but not naive. I knew that she could never afford all of these luxuries on the wages of the part-time job she had convinced the courts that she held.

"So what's the real story?" I asked Trish, not even about to beat around the bush, as I flopped down on the couch.

"What are you talking about, girl?" She raised her arms and then let them fall to her side. "Look around, little mama. This is the real story." She sat down next to me, admiring her apartment with pride. "I'm living the life, and now that you're here with me, everything is perfect." Her toned turned serious as she looked at me. "We're all we have, Summer. Just you and me. And I wanted you to come home to something nice—to something better than you had while in the system, and something better than you had before you went into the system."

I could feel where big sis was coming from, but that still didn't answer my question. "I know, but what are you doing to get all of this?" I looked around again. "I mean, it's tight up in here, and I can look around and tell that this is the real deal—the real story." I turned my attention back to Trish. "But my question is how the heck did you get it written?"

Trish chuckled. She knew I wasn't going to back down. She leaned back against the couch, sighed, and then began to speak. "I met Boss about six months ago. We hit it off and started dating. Boss owns his own business." She squirmed just slightly. Not too much, but enough for me to notice. "I help him out with his business, and he pays me well," she bragged.

"His business?" I quizzed. "By that you mean drugs?"

She smacked her lips and then stood up. "I don't know, Summer. Unlike your nosy behind, I don't ask too many questions. I just pick up packages for him and sometimes he has me drop things off. He told me never to look inside the bags, so I don't," Trish responded with a shrug. "Hungry? Want something to eat?" she asked, quickly changing the subject.

I couldn't believe that Trish was involved with a guy like Boss. I didn't know him, but already I didn't like him.

I rubbed my hand up and down the soft suede. A sista had to admit I liked the benefits . . . to a degree. And I was grateful to be in a place I could truly call home, back with the only family I had. So I decided to drop the subject, following Trish's example.

"I'm starved." I stood up and stretched. "But first things first. Where's my room?" I asked with a smile.

"Come on, let me show you," Trish said, returning the smile. I could tell she was relieved I'd let the subject of Boss and his business go. I could also tell that she knew more about Boss's business than she was willing to share with me. But I was sure I'd find out more than I needed to know sooner than I needed to know it.

Trish led me down the hallway to a door that had a paper sign with my name written on it in colorful bubble letters. I laughed as I tore the sign off the door.

"Bubble letters, Trish? I'm not eight anymore." I waved the sign with a huge smile on my face.

"I know. I just forget sometimes. You're my baby sis," she replied, throwing her arm around my shoulders.

I shook my head and opened the door. Shocked was the only way to describe my reaction. Trish had definitely hooked me up. My champagne- and pink-colored bedspread fit perfectly on the oak queen sized bed. I had a plasma television on the wall, a computer sitting in the corner, and a walk-in closet with all of the latest teen fashions. I turned to Trish after checking out the contents of my closet.

"Looks like somebody already did all the shopping," I said.

Trish winked. "You didn't think I'd hook up our place but not my little sis's wardrobe, did you?"

I fingered some of the outfits in the closet, thinking how I was going be the best dressed girl at Cass High School. Today was the last day of summer break, so I would get a fresh start on the new school year without having to try to fit in in the middle of the year when all the cliques have already been formed.

I know it sounds crazy, but I was actually excited about starting school. I would finally get to attend a regular public school again instead of just those classes at the group home facility. I'll never know why they have the word *home* as part of it. It felt more like a prison to me—a boot camp.

"What's that?" I asked Trish after exiting the closet and pointing to a closed door. "Another closet?"

"Girl, no." She walked over and opened the door. "That's your bathroom."

I had to be dreaming. Maybe I had nodded off into la- la land while I was standing there waiting for the judge to make his decision, and any minute now Trish was going to nudge my shoulder and bring me back to reality.

"Well, do you like it?" Trish asked, putting her hand on my shoulder. I just stood there frozen. "Well? Hello. Earth to Summer." She shook my shoulder.

I came out of my daze and looked around. Nope, I wasn't dreaming. I was still right there in my own bedroom with my own private bath. "Like it? Sis, I love it," I said, walking past her and into the bathroom that was decorated in lilac and cream décor. I was on cloud nine. "Thank you, Trish," I said appreciatively as I walked over and bear hugged her so tightly that she couldn't breathe.

"Okay, okay," she screamed for mercy. "You get settled in here. I'm going to whip you up a sandwich and chips. Then I have to go meet back up with Boss, but make yourself at home." Trish turned to exit my room.

"You're leaving?" I asked, my tone laced in full disappointment.

"You heard him say he needed to get with me," she replied.

I stomped over to the bed and sat down. "Does he realize how long it's been since I've spent time with you? I've waited years for this day to come. And now you're telling me that your business with him can't wait?" I folded my arms pretzel-style, waiting impatiently for Trish to reply.

"Calm down, Summer. You're home now. We have all the time in the world to spend together. I'll be back later, and I promise I won't be long," she tried to assure me. "I'm working on something that will make a better life for both of us." She looked around my room. "This right here, baby girl, you ain't seen nothing yet. But you have to trust me on this, okay?"

"Yeah, okay," I replied. I was disappointed, but realized that whether I wanted her to or not, Trish was leaving, so I may as well chill out.

"Aww, don't look so sad," Trish said as she walked

over to my bed and teased me by pinching my check. I playfully shooed her hand away as I cracked a smile.

"But seriously, Summer. I'll be back. You don't have to worry about me ever leaving you again. You got that?"

I nodded. Trish made her way out of my room. Before I heard the front door close, I'd heard Trish clinking and clanking in the kitchen, preparing my food.

When Trish left, I couldn't get out of my old Goodwill clothes fast enough. I hopped in the shower and took the best shower that I'd taken in years. After I was done, I walked over to the oak chest and began fumbling through drawers. Trish had everything I needed from bras to panties to socks to sleepwear. Instead of putting on clothes, I decided to put on a pair of the expensive-looking pajamas Trish had waiting in the drawers for me.

After slipping into my PJs, I went to the kitchen. I spotted the plate Trish had left me with a turkey sandwich, chips, and a pickle on it. I walked over to the fridge and opened it in search of something to wash my food down. The fridge was fully stocked. The beverage choices seemed unlimited, from juice to soda to bottled water to Vitamin Water, milk, chocolate milk, etc . . . I decided on a Strawberry Crush. I scarfed down my food and drink and then went back to my room and lay down in my bed.

The six hundred thread count sheets and silk pajamas were a deadly combination and I was out like a light almost as soon as my head hit the pillow. It felt so good to be home and I knew this was only just the beginning.

Chapter Two

"Summer"

When I awoke it was nighttime and the darkness had enveloped my room like a plague. I was disoriented at first; hadn't a clue as to where I was. I was so used to waking up to the sound of other girls around me that the silence felt strange, but I liked it all the same. I noticed a light shining under the crack of my closed bedroom door and I got up, hoping that Trish had come home. I opened the door, stepped into the hallway, and then made my way to Trish's room.

"What are you doing?" I asked as I leaned against her door frame.

She jumped and knocked over the bag that was on

her bed, causing a stack of money to spill out onto the floor.

"Dang it, Summer, you scared the snot out of me," she said as she got on her knees and began to scoop the money up from the floor.

My eyes bulged as I looked at all those dead men who were being honored by having their faces printed on U.S. currency. "Where did you get all of that money?" I asked as I stared incredulously at the array of denominations at her feet.

"I've been saving it," Trish answered as she pulled up two wooden floor panels and stuffed the bag inside. She then snapped the panels back in place.

"Well, why don't you put it in the bank or something? It's not safe to have all of that money lying around the house," I stated seriously.

"You're the only other person who knows about it. So keep it that way, okay?" Trish instructed.

"Yeah, no problem."

Trish looked up at me suspiciously. "And don't get any cute ideas either. If you need something, all you have to do is ask. You hear me?"

"Girl, please." I smacked my lips. "Like I'ma take from my own sister. I should be offended, but lucky for you that I love you so much, I'm not." I shrugged. "Besides, if I had that kind of money in my bedroom floorboards, I don't think I'd trust you." I had a sudden thought then said to Trish. "I don't have that kind of money in my bedroom floorboards . . . do I?"

"You wish." Trish chuckled.

"A girl can be hopeful, can't she?"

"Keep hope alive, little sis. Keep hope alive. Just keep your paws off my hard-earned savings."

"Savings?" My voice was filled with doubt, but I left it alone.

In a firm tone, Trish once again affirmed, "Savings."

I knew that Trish wasn't telling me the entire story, but from the look on her face and the tone of her voice, the conversation was obviously over.

"Get dressed. We're going out tonight," Trish said as she headed over to her own walk-in closet, which made mine look like a matchbox.

"Going out. It's the middle of the week. What about school?" I asked, knowing I had to report for my first day of classes tomorrow.

"Girl, I'm your sister, not your parent. You don't have to ever go to school if you don't want to. Boss is throwing an end of the summer block party. There will be people your age there, and I bet you they ain't worried about school," Trish urged.

I couldn't wait to show of my threads at school tomorrow. I'd already picked out exactly which outfit I wanted to wear. The last thing I needed was for my clothes to be all that, but my face and hair to be looking a hot mess 'cause I was out kickin' it all night. On the flip side, just hours ago, wasn't it me who was pouting about wanting to spend time with Trish? Well, I guess this was my opportunity, and I couldn't pass it up.

"I'll go out, but I'm not staying out all night, because I'm going to school tomorrow," I confirmed.

Trish laughed and replied, "Yeah, I remember when I first got out of the group home too. I went to school every day, just glad I was in a regular school environment, meeting new friends and stuff. That got old real quick though."

"Well, it won't get old for me," I assured her. "A sista like me got college bound dreams so that one day I can have a place like this."

"Think about it, little sis. I didn't go to college, and I have a place like this." Trish had a point. I stood there and took in her words before she interrupted my thoughts. "Anyway, later with this talk about school." She grabbed me by the hand. "Here, come in the kitchen. I've got something for you."

I smiled as Trish led me into the kitchen. When she turned on the kitchen light, I covered my mouth in surprise. There was a bouquet of helium birthday balloons tied to one of the chairs in the dining area, and a decorated sheet cake sat on the table. Trish smiled as she walked over and lit the big number-sixteen candle and began to sing.

"Happy birthday to you. You're older and uglier too. You look like a monkey and you smell like a zoo, but even though you're stinky, I still do love you!"

Her song was off key, but I loved her for it. It was the goofy version that our mama used to sing to us each year. It brought tears to my eyes and I fanned them away.

"Quit crying and make a wish," Trish urged.

For a minute, standing there looking at Trish, she reminded me of Mama. I felt the same care and love coming from her as I had from Mama when she was alive. Although Trish could never replace Mama, she was the greatest sister in the world.

I took a deep breath and inhaled. *I wish that Trish and I will always be together,* I thought before I blew out the candle. Trish began to applaud.

"Thank you, Trish," I said. "Thank you so much."

"Don't thank me, Summer. This is what I'm supposed to do. You're my baby sister, and I wanted to show you that you're special," she replied. She grabbed the digital camera that was sitting on the countertop and said, "Now picture time."

I leaned my face down by the cake and Trish took a

picture. Next, she came over and stood by me. We got close to each other and she stretched her arm and snapped the photo.

"Let me get you a knife so you can cut the first piece," Trish said as she went over to the drawer next to the dishwasher and pulled out a knife. She then reached up to the cabinet above the dishwasher and pulled out two small plates.

I cut into the chocolate cake, my favorite flavor. I placed a piece on Trish's plate and the piece with the rose on my plate. The birthday honoree always gets the rose.

We sat down and had cake together as we laughed and caught up. It had been so long since my sister and I had been around each other for more than thirty minutes. That was the lousy time she was permitted to come see me at the home two days a week. She never missed a visit, might I add, but it felt great now to just kick back and be with her on our own time, with no rules attached and without having to watch the clock.

Trish stood and began to clear our plates from the table. "Okay, now go get dressed. We're leaving in a little bit."

A half hour later, I was dressed and ready to go. The Baby Phat jeans, black American Eagle flats, and black camisole I wore were trendy, and I was defi-

nitely feeling myself. It was the same out[...]
on wearing to school the next day, so I'[...]
out something else in the morning. Th[...]
just begging to be worn ASAP.

When Trish put my thick, long hair in [...], I
went from bummy to ghetto chic. I loved my look,
and I quickly discovered that I was conceited. I could
not stop looking at myself in the mirror. Trish gave
me two large, diamond-studded hoop earrings.

"Are these real?" I asked in disbelief as I saw the
light in the room dance inside the diamonds.

"We don't wear fake stuff around here," Trish
replied. "Only the real thing, baby." She twisted her
lips and I could see where I'd inherited my conceit.
"Let's go. It's time for you to make your debut."

Trish grabbed her purse and keys, then locked the
door behind us. We made our way to a nice 2009
Chevy Impala. It wasn't as elaborate as Boss's truck,
but I had to admit that Trish was doing well for herself. I still wasn't feeling how my sister made her
money, but she was definitely living a comfortable
lifestyle and she was willing to share it with me, so I
couldn't really hate on her.

We drove for about fifteen minutes or so and then
pulled onto Runyon Drive. The streetlights illumi-
nated the people gathered outside. The block was full
of tricked-out, old school cars, and everybody seemed

to be having a good time. Trish parked in the driveway of the biggest house on the street. I assumed it was where Boss lived.

We got out, and Boss greeted Trish with a kiss to the cheek. He had a Heineken bottle in one hand and draped his other arm around Trish.

"What up, baby?" he asked her.

"You," Trish replied as she happily took her place on his arm, looking like a well placed trophy in her hot pink Baby Phat tee with a gold Baby Phat embossed emblem and painted on Baby Phat jeans. She was sportin' hot pink patent leather pumps the exact color of the shirt. Kimora Lee couldn't have represented Baby Phat any better herself.

"What's good, Summer?" Boss acknowledged me. I nodded in return. I didn't want to completely ignore him, but I definitely planned on keeping him at a distance until I could figure him out. "Yo, I know a couple people that go to your school. I can have one of my little dudes show you around or something. I know you've been away for a while," he said.

"Yeah, thanks, but I'm good. I don't want my business all over school before I get there," I replied with a half smile.

"Yo, Jus!" Boss called out like he hadn't just heard me decline his offer. A brown-skinned boy with a medium build and a charming smile sauntered over to Boss, pulling up his pants to keep them from falling even lower than they already were. "I want you to meet somebody."

Didn't I just tell him that I did not want to meet his friends? The look I shot to Trish said it all. Was her man hard of hearing or something?

"This is my li'l man, Jus. Jus, this is Trish's sister, Summer. She's starting at Cass tomorrow," Boss stated.

Jus turned his attention to me. "What up?" he greeted as he looked me up and down, surveying my appearance.

I gave him the head nod too and then turned to Trish and said, "Is there something to drink around here?"

Boss answered for my sister. "Yeah, it's food and drinks in the backyard. Jus will show you around." He walked off with Trish and left me standing beside his friend. Now it was very clear why he played deaf. He was just trying to pawn me off on someone while he chilled with my sister. I hoped Boss didn't think for one minute he was going to come between Trish and me. That was a no-no. I could see now we might bump heads sooner or later. From the looks of things, it would probably be sooner. Much sooner.

Jus chuckled a little bit.

"What's so funny?" I asked.

"Nothing. You still want that drink?" he asked as he offered his beer to me.

I frowned and shook my head. "Yeah, but a regular drink . . . like water or juice or something," I said.

Once again, Jus gave me the once over and then chuckled. I couldn't wait to find out just what this dude thought was so funny. But for now, I was parched. I needed that drink.

I crossed my arms as I followed Jus to the backyard, where there was a barbecue grill going and a table full of food and beverages set up. There were people all over smoking and drinking.

I helped myself as I surveyed my surroundings. *I am going to kill Trish for leaving me by myself*, I thought. It was uncomfortable being around so many people I didn't know, and I was already ready to leave.

"Why haven't I seen you around?" Jus asked.

I shrugged. I hadn't decided what I would tell people about my past. I knew whatever I came up with would be better than the truth.

"How old are you?" he asked. It seemed to me that if I didn't answer his first question, then it would have been common sense for him not to ask me any more.

"Why do you ask so many questions?" I took a drink of the ice cold bottled water I'd located in a cooler next to the table of drinks.

"You seem a little uptight, ma. I'm just trying to loosen you up," he said. "You know, make small talk."

"I'm not uptight. I just don't know you like that for you to be all up in my business," I responded.

He huffed and shook his head before taking a drink of his beer. A little part of me felt bad for being so hard. I decided to bring it down a notch and, like he said, make small talk.

"So, you go to Cass?"

"Oh, now you in my business?" he joked.

"No, I was just wondering. Boss said that some people he knows go there."

"I graduated last year," he stated.

I saw Trish emerge through the crowd and I motioned her over.

"Having fun, little sis?" she asked, all happy-go-lucky as she made her way over to me.

"I'm not really feeling this," I said when she was within earshot. "Can you take me back to the apartment?"

"We just got here," she said. She looked over at Jus suspiciously "Is everything okay?" She was now whispering. "He bothering you? He ain't bothering you, is he? Because if he is—"

"No, he's not bothering me," I said between gritted teeth, trying to calm her down. "I'm fine. I'm just not comfortable here," I explained.

Trish's shoulders seemed to relax as if relieved she wasn't about to have to be about some drama. "It's your birthday, Summer. You're sixteen, girl! Relax and have a good time," she said.

I could tell she was trying her best to convince me to stay, but I was straight on that. I just wanted to go back to the apartment. It was my first day of freedom, and all I'd wanted to do was spend it with my big sis. Not my big sis, Boss, Jus, and all these other fools. And since it didn't look like I was gonna get any me and Trish time, then I'd settle for just some me time.

Truth be told, I think I was a little bit overwhelmed by everything that was going on around me. I felt like I would get in trouble for being out too late. It was almost like I was still living by the rules of the group home. I hated that place and did not want to go back, so if I had to be strict on myself, then so be it. I wasn't about to give the system a reason to snatch me away from my family again. I gave Trish an exasperated sigh and looked at her in irritation.

She sighed and looked at her watch. "Summer, I've got to stay here with Boss." She looked toward Jus. "Do you mind dropping my sister off at my place?" she asked him.

"Trish!" I whispered harshly, once again between gritted teeth. I did not know Jus from Adam and did not feel like going through the trouble of getting to know him.

"What?" She looked at me like I was crazy. "You said you wanted to go home. Well, Jus will take you," she said as if she didn't see anything wrong with me hopping into the car with a complete stranger. I don't care whether she knew him or not; whether he was Boss's people or not. He was nobody to me.

"Yeah, I'll drop her off. It ain't nothing but a thang," Jus replied coolly with an attractive smirk.

"See, now, there's your ride home," Trish said, "unless you've had a change of heart and want to stay and hang out."

If I didn't know any better, that was Trish's entire purpose in asking Jus to take me home: to get me to change my mind and stay.

"Fine," I snapped, rolling my eyes.

"Fine, you'll stay?" Trish asked excitedly.

"No, fine I'll ride with Jus." I looked over to Jus and asked, "Where's your car?"

Trish gave me a hug good-bye and walked away.

"It's at home," he answered.

"Home? Then how are you supposed to take me home?" I asked, growing tired of his games. "Give me a piggy back ride on your back or something?"

"No," he replied and then pointed to a black-and-silver Ninja motorcycle. "I'ma let you ride on that."

He looked at me with this smart-alec grin on his face. "That is unless you want to drive it. I don't mind being taken for a ride."

I smacked my lips at his lame lines. Besides, there was no way he was getting me on the back of that thing.

"Uh-uh, no!" I protested firmly.

"That's fine with me," Jus replied as he headed over to his bike. "I mean, you could always stay here and wait on Trish."

I looked back at Trish, who had taken her place on Boss's arm. "But she usually stays the night," he said while holding out a passenger helmet for me. He was obviously amused by my dilemma.

My first day of freedom was not going as expected. "Whatever. Just go slow," I stated as I stomped over to his bike and snatched the helmet from his hands.

He helped me put it on before he mounted the bike like it was a horse and he was in a rodeo. He then looked over his shoulder at me. He held out his hand, and I reluctantly placed mine in his and allowed him to aid me as I mounted the back of the bike.

He started the bike and my nerves went crazy. "Remember, go slow."

"There's no such thing as slow on a motorcycle. Just hold on tight," he said.

I closed my eyes and felt the kickback of the engine as he revved up and pulled off. He jumped on the expressway and I held on around his waist for dear life as he weaved in and out of traffic. We arrived in downtown Detroit in no time, and I was home in less than ten minutes.

"Well, here you are," Jus said as he pulled up in front of the apartment building and stood idle.

I carefully got off the bike and removed the helmet. As I stood there, I could still feel the vibration from all that roaring metal that had been between my legs. I thought my legs were going to turn to jelly and I'd puddle to the ground. I gathered my composure and then returned the helmet to Jus. "Thanks," I said.

"Anytime," he responded as he watched me walk away. "Oh yeah, Summer!" he called out. I turned around to see what he wanted. "Happy birthday, ma." The words bounced off of the wind as he revved his engine, making his back tire burn into the cement before pulling away.

I rolled my eyes and entered the building, grateful to be home . . . alive. One thing was for sure: Trish's crowd was definitely not my crowd. Trish had changed a lot since the last time I had seen her. She was different, but then again, so was I.

Chapter Three

"Summer"

When I walked into the school the next day, I felt like I had a neon sign on my head that said NEW GIRL. Everybody seemed to watch me as I passed through the hallways. My Somerset Ferragamo outfit definitely stood out from the Baby Phat jeans and Pelle Pelle hookups that everybody else wore. *Trish would pick me out an entire wardrobe of high fashion designers,* I thought, realizing that I stuck out like a sore thumb.

Most of the girls my age wore Air Force Ones, or Air Maxes. The girls with little feet could get away with Jordans, and here I was high-heeling it up in skinny jeans and a silk blouse to match. Don't get me wrong, I was that girl and I looked good, but I was going to have to downgrade for sure. Haters already hated for no reason at all, so why add to the drama by giving them all the more reason to hate?

I swear as I walked down the hall it was the click, click, click of my shoes that drew even more attention. I made a mental note right then and there that heels would become flip flops, and as soon possible, I would cop myself a couple pair of kicks. I could already see the intimidation on the popular girls' faces. I could tell the popular girls by the way they stood in the hall, as if where they stood was a special spot that no one else was deemed worthy to even come near. They were all wondering how long it would take me to snatch their spots as the "it girl" in school, but I was not there for all that. I was just trying to blend.

Because of my dysfunctional upbringing, I had been different most of my life. For once, I just wanted to feel regular, do regular things, and have regular teenage problems. Most girls my age wanted to be grown up. They could not wait to get out in the real world and go buck wild, but me, I had been there and done that. I'd been in the so-called real world. Now all I wanted to do was worry about things girls my age worried about; like what boy liked me. I yearned to know what it felt like to be on the cheerleading team. I wanted to stress out about what to wear to homecoming dances and prom. Yep, I wanted to be your everyday, around the way girl from the hood. Simply stated, I just wanted to be young.

I managed to find my way to my first class on my own. For some reason, I didn't feel the love in the air from my fellow peers enough to ask them for any assistance. I was elated when I finally stepped into my English class before the tardy bell had sounded. And the bonus was that English was my favorite subject.

Although I really wanted to take a seat in the front row, I sat in the back because I did not want to be one of those new kids who tried to brown nose the teachers by sitting up front and answering all the questions. In fact, I probably would not know the answers to most of the questions anyway, so I quickly decided that the back seat was the best place for me. My seat selection did not really matter, however, because as soon as the bell rang, my teacher put me on blast.

"Welcome back, everyone. My name is Mrs. Williams, and I recognize most of you from seeing you around the school last year. We do have one new student, however. Is Summer Flynt here?" she asked.

I closed my eyes and inhaled deeply as my heart sped up. I was not nervous, but the whole "stand up and state your name and tell the class a little bit about yourself" routine was so not necessary. Why all teachers feel the need to introduce new students to the world is beyond me. There needed to be a rule or something prohibiting that. If I wanted everybody to know my name, I would have worn a name tag or something.

"Summer Flynt?" she called out again. I rolled my eyes and stood up reluctantly. "Oh, there you are. Why don't you introduce yourself to the class? Tell us something like where you're from, or what school you're transferring from."

I waved shyly and then stuck my fingers in my belt loops. "Hey, everybody, I'm Summer." I paused and then shrugged my shoulders. "That's about it," I stated. I hoped she did not expect a speech because that simple hello was as good as it was going to get. "Oh, and I'm from . . . around." I quickly sat in my seat and prayed I didn't have to do this in every class.

All of my classes seemed to go by pretty slowly. With it being the first day back to school, all we pretty much did was get assigned seats, fill out some papers, go over class rules and future assignments, etc. . . . By lunch, I was bored out of my mind.

Finding my way to the cafeteria wasn't that difficult. I simply followed the drove of people chatting away. I walked into the cafeteria and got in the long line of students. The lunch line seemed to go even slower than my classes did. Perhaps the lunch lady was running down the cafeteria rules to everybody. I don't know what the hold up was, but I do know that I almost dozed off until a voice came out of nowhere.

"You're the new girl everybody's talking about, right?" a girl beside me asked.

I looked her up and down. She was one of the few girls that didn't have on jeans. The business-style capri pants and wraparound mini-shirt she wore signaled that she had style. And the Movado watch on her wrist indicated that her parents had money.

"I didn't know I was the talk of the school," I commented.

"It's not all bad. Everybody's just wondering who you are. No one has seen you around before," another girl who looked exactly like the first girl stated. It would have been dumb to ask them if they were related. It was obvious that the two were twin sisters. I stared at each of them as we scooted up a bit in the line. There was absolutely no telling the two apart. They had to be identical.

"Don't even try to find a difference. None of our friends can tell us apart," the first girl said after noticing how hard I was staring and how my eyes were darting back and forth between the two of them. "I'm Mya," she introduced. "This is my sister, Tara."

"Summer," I replied as I lifted my tray.

"You can sit at our table," she stated matter-of-factly, as if I would be crazy to say no.

I figured that her clique was probably the most popular one out of all the cliques—smart, stylish, and cute. We made our way through the line and I let them lead the way to the table. The way that the other students showed mad love to the twins when they walked by told me that they were like royalty at Cass.

Tara seemed to be the more reserved of the twins. She didn't say much, and received much less attention than Mya. I peeped how everyone spoke to both girls, but they always seemed to speak to Mya first, then, as if looking for her shadow, they'd speak to Tara.

Tara may not have been as front and center as Mya, but she was no less beautiful. She just seemed shy, but with a sister like Mya who demanded attention, I guess she didn't have a choice but to take the back seat.

After the girls said all of their hellos to everyone, we finally made it over to the lunch table, where I was introduced to another member of their group.

"Latina, this is Summer . . . Summer, Latina," Mya introduced.

The girl gave me a quick hey, and I hit her with the head nod then took a seat.

"So, where you from?" Mya asked me.

Here comes the question, I thought. "Atlanta," I said

aloud. I figured if I told them I was from some other place, they wouldn't ask too much more about me and my life here in Michigan. Just like Trish said, it was new beginnings. The old life was history.

The questions continued to flow out of the girls' mouths like water. Obviously, I had said the wrong city, because it piqued their interest to the point that by the end of the lunch hour, I'd been forced to make up an entire life.

When they asked about my moms and pops and what they did for a living, I told them that my parents had let me move up to Detroit from Atlanta to live with my older sister. At least I'd told some truth; I did live with my older sister. All the girls thought that it was the coolest thing they had ever heard, me living with my sister who wasn't really that much older than us.

Mya automatically declared that my spot would be their new hangout, because I had no parental supervision and I'd made my sister seem so cool and down to earth—especially when I told them one other truth about how Trish wasn't worried about me showing up for school the first day. I told them how she was going to let me hang out all night the night before the first day of school, but I chose to call it an early night. It seemed like the truths were getting me into more trouble than the lies.

I didn't promise the girls anything as far as Trish being down with allowing her place to be the hang-out. I mean, keeping it real, I didn't even know if I liked these chicks yet, but at least they believed my story. All I had to do was make sure I remembered everything that I had told them.

After lunch, the rest of the afternoon went by even more slowly than the morning had. When the final bell rang, I was relieved beyond words. I decided that I'd take Trish up on her offer about not being so serious about school, and that school would definitely not be an everyday thing. I would come enough to keep the courts and the counselors off of my back, but I'd made up my mind that I could not handle the charade every day.

High school is like a big fashion show with a whole bunch of critics. Any and everybody always has something to say about somebody. That was not my type of scene. Back at the home, everybody wore the same charity, thrift store hand-me-down stuff. It was regulation that we couldn't possess expensive stuff up in there because the home wouldn't be responsible for theft. We all mirrored each other. So if we talked about one person, then we might as well have been talking about ourselves.

Things at Cass were definitely not how things were back at the home, and I just couldn't be down with it.

I was beginning to think I was anti-social. If it wasn't for Mya and her few clique members I chose to interact with, I'd probably even be deemed as a nerd. But everyone knew that if you were seen with Mya, then you were far from a nerd.

One day after school, I walked out of the building and noticed four cars sitting in the parking lot. Three of the cars were hooked-up old school cars—a.k.a. the poor man's Bentley—but there was one 2009 Audi sitting on shiny, spinning rims. The beat from the custom speakers demanded attention, and most of the girls didn't have a problem showing how impressed they were. They paraded past the cars, hoping to grab the interest of the boys inside.

I felt a hand on my shoulder and turned around to find Mya standing behind me.

"That's who I'm trying to get with," she stated, pointing at whoever was behind the tinted windows of the Audi.

"What's stopping you?" I asked, squinting my eyes like I was Superman or something and if I looked long and hard enough I would eventually be able to see through the windows. It wasn't as if I was interested; I just wanted to see what all the fuss was about.

"All them dudes . . ." Mya pointed to the stand out vehicles and then continued. "They don't mess with high school chicks. They get money all over the city.

The dudes in the old cars are always driving around stunting. Showing off their whips," Mya explained. "The one in the Audi don't show his face much. I've seen him around a couple times, but he is stuck up. He's fine as ever, though, so I'd get with him." She licked her lips. "Heck, with all the money they be gettin', I'd get with any of them. You feel me?" She chuckled as she bumped my shoulder, trying to get me to co-sign.

I just shook my head. "Well, I got to go. I'll see y'all tomorrow," I said as I spotted the rest of her crew rolling up behind her. "My bus is about to leave."

"I'll give you a ride," Mya stated. "Where you live?"

I hesitated. I hadn't told the girls exactly where I lived, hoping that would keep them from staying true to their word and making my spot the hangout. But they were bound to find out, so I figured why not now; especially when the bus was looking so cramped and I knew it would be a miserable ride home. "Downtown, on the bank," I replied.

"Yeah, I got you. Come on," Mya offered.

I followed Mya, Tara, and Latina through the parking lot. It was obvious that all of them were trying their hardest to turn the heads of the occupants of those cars. I once again shook my head and switched my way past the row of cars.

"Ay, yo, let me holla at you for a minute, shorty," a

voice stated as we all walked by. I kept it moving because I knew dude wasn't talking to me.

"Hey, Summer, I think he's talking to you," Tara said, halting my steps.

"Shut up, Tara. He doesn't know her. She's new," Mya said harshly. There was just a hint of jealousy in her voice. She probably figured if anybody was going to get hollered at by one of those dudes, it would be her.

I turned around to see who it was that was calling out for one of us, but the window was rolled up too high for me to see the driver's face. The small crack in the window revealed nothing.

"Yo, Summer, come here," the voice called out again, this time with a bit of impatience in his voice.

Mya, Tara, and Latina's chins dropped to their chests when they heard dude call me by name. Now it was clear exactly who the mystery man behind the wheel was checking for. The crew looked at me like I was crazy. I shrugged and then walked over to the car. The window came down, and behind the wheel sat Jus, poised and attractive in jeans, a white T-shirt, and a red fitted Phillies cap on his head.

"What up?" he asked.

"What up?" I replied. I couldn't believe that this was the boy that everybody was tripping on. I had to admit he was fine, but he wasn't all that. I didn't like the company he kept. If he was in the same business as Boss, then in my opinion, that alone brought his stock down.

"Get in," he ordered like he was the boss of me.

"For what?" I frowned as I crossed my arms, cocked one hip to the side, and let my bookbag hang from one arm. Jus looked me up and down. He was eyeing me like I was a steak and he hadn't eaten in days. "What are you looking at?" I asked him.

"Just admiring the view," he commented. "Come take a ride with your man." He popped the locks.

I looked back at my new friends, if that's what you want to call them. They were glued on the interaction taking place before their eyes, as if Jus and I were the new Jay-Z and Beyoncé video.

"I don't know you like that," I replied coyly. "Besides, I already have a ride." I looked over my shoulder. He followed my eyes to see Mya and the girls waiting on me.

"A'ight then, I'll check you later," he said as he rolled up the window and pulled away.

My eyes stayed glued on the vehicle until it was out of sight. I could feel eyes burning a hole through me the same way my eyes were burning a hole through Jus's Audi. I did all I could not to let the smile that was yearning to escape my lips break through. For some reason, now that I knew that every other girl in school wanted the man behind the wheel, Jus didn't seem like he could be so bad after all. He still wasn't my type though, so I wiped off the little bit of smile that had forced its way through and walked back over to the girls.

"You didn't tell me you knew him! How do you know him?" Mya grilled.

"He was feeling you, girl," Latina added. "Y'all kickin' it or something? How you just happen to stumble upon his fine self?"

"I don't know him like that. I just met him a few nights ago; the day before school started," I commented. "But anyway, y'all ready to go?" I asked with a nonchalant tone. I knew that Jus had upgraded my status at Cass by acknowledging that he knew me, and the fact that he had that much power made me wonder exactly what type of crowd my sister was surrounded by.

We approached Mya's car and Tara went straight for the front while I started to get inside the backseat along with Latina. That's when Mya stopped me.

"Uh-uh, Summer, you ride shotgun. Tara can sit in the back," she instructed. She looked over at her sister and nodded toward the backseat.

"What do you mean I can get in the back? This is my car too. How you gon' put me in the backseat of my own dang car?" Tara protested. That was the most attitude I had ever seen Tara possess. Heck, I didn't even know the girl had it in her. Shows we can't always judge a book by its cover.

"It's cool," I stated smoothly. "I'm just glad you guys are giving me a ride. I can ride in the back."

"No, you'll ride in the front," Mya said, cutting her eyes at her sister. She was not asking, she was telling.

I hesitated, not wanting to start a fight between the twins, but Tara went on and got in the back, so I got in the front. Mya pumped up her sound system and we headed out of the school parking lot.

The first week of school hadn't been all that bad. But just like I had suspected, I eventually became "that girl," and all of my new friends were the baddest chicks in school. I was teen royalty, and I owed it all to Jus.

Chapter Four

"Summer"

School was perfect. I'd changed my mind about not making it an every day thing. As a matter of fact, a lot had changed, including myself. Whatever shell I thought I was going to crawl up inside and live in at Cass, I quickly shed. Something inside of me craved to be that front and center chick.

When I was at school, I felt important. Summer became a household name. Haters spoke it on the daily, and friends admired me when I was not around. Most importantly, all the guys knew who I was. Some even placed bets on who could make me his girl first, as if that would ever happen. I learned quickly that dating a boy my age was not the thing to do. High school boys were immature, and my crew didn't have time to play childish games.

Over the next couple of months, Mya, Tara, and Latina became the clique that I rocked with. We became so close that I insisted my spot be the crew's official hangout, always inviting them over. The four of us did everything together, and they loved staying the night at my house because it was like we were grown. Trish was cool and we didn't have rules or a curfew. Mya and 'em always wanted to chill with Trish because she stayed around Boss, Jus, and their crew. I wasn't feeling that too much, but I went with the flow.

Although I had an entire school of people who I considered associates and Mya and I were the tightest, Trish was my best friend. She was my girl, and no matter what, I could never replace her. She was not around a lot because she was always handling business with Boss, but when she was home, all of her time was spent with me.

Trish resembled our mother so much that it was almost like having Mama around again. For the first time in a long time I was happy. The sound of the *DING! DING!* still hadn't left my dreams at night yet, and I still thought of Mama's death often, but just the simple fact that I was around Trish again and we were a family made it a little bit better. *There's always a rainbow after the storm,* Mama used to say to me when I was younger.

My thoughts were interrupted by the doorbell. I heard the click-clack of Trish's stilettos on the hardwood floor heading to the door, and then moments later, I heard the voices of my girls as they entered the apartment.

Latina burst into my room first. She wore a white bubble RocaWear coat that matched her snow white boots. We all had the same outfit. We were sixteen, so we didn't realize how corny it was for us all to dress alike.

"Hey, chick," she greeted as she plopped down on my bed.

"Hey, y'all," I replied as Mya and Tara entered behind her.

"We're going to see your boo," Mya stated.

"Girl, please, don't nobody like that boy," I protested, referring to Jus. He always flirted with me when we all got together, and although it was flattering, I knew in my heart that he was not for me.

He was not my type, but the girl in me just loved the attention he gave me and the admiration it brought about from others. Jus was never disrespectful or anything around me, but I felt that people hung around people who they were similar to—you know, cut from the same cloth. He hung around Boss on a regular basis. Enough said.

"He *is* feeling you and you know it," Tara added. She usually kept to herself, and for her to add a comment, I knew that she really thought Latina was right.

"Whatever. Let's get out of here before Trish leaves us," I said as I grabbed my white coat and walked out the door.

Corn rows had become my trademark. Each girl in the clique had her own trademark. My braids were usually done to the side so that they hung over one shoulder. Mya and Tara wore their shoulder-length hair wrapped in layers, and Latina usually wore a cute ponytail. We were all fly and we knew it. It was like after the first day of school we all knew we were meant to be cool. They accepted me like I was an original member. We were too much alike and had too many things in common to dislike one another, and although I think Mya was a bit salty that she had some competition now, she knew that it was smarter to clique up rather than beef out with one another.

As the girls and I made our way to the living room, Trish stepped out of her room wearing a black Gucci dress with matching stiletto leather boots and a casual jean jacket.

"Your sister is so fly," Tara stated under her breath

as she watched Trish head our way. It was almost as if Tara was in a daze or something.

Mya snapped her fingers in front of Tara's face. "Dang, Tara. Snap out of it and get off her jock," Mya scoffed with sarcasm. She hated when she wasn't the center of attention.

"Quit hating, Mya. You know my sis is fly. Where you think I get it from?" I bragged as I began to strut back and forth, twitching my hips.

She rolled her eyes and we followed Trish outside. I rode with my sister, and my friends followed close behind as we headed toward Boss's crib. He was having a little get-together, nothing too big. It was just a wing-ding party to watch the Lions play on TV. I didn't really want to go, but my girls were willing to do anything to be close to Boss and his crew. They were such groupies, but I loved them, so whatever.

We arrived at Boss's spot and walked into the house using the side door. We went straight down the flight of steps that led to the finished basement.

Everybody greeted Trish, me, and my girls. We were common faces around there now, so we mixed and mingled casually as we conversed and cracked jokes with people we knew. Mostly everyone there was older than us. They were all Trish's age, which meant that there was plenty of alcohol to go around. My girls and

I turned down the drinks. It wasn't that we were goody-two-shoes. For me, the smell of liquor wasn't enticing, so I never had the urge to drink. As far as my girls were concerned, if they had been spending the night at my place, they probably would have gotten their drink on, but tonight they had to go home to their parents, so they knew they had to stay sober. But even without the devil's juice, we were having a good time.

Everything was all good until about an hour later, when it was apparent that Boss had had way too much to drink and decided to get stupid with my sister. He was possessive and controlling off the bat, not to mention jealous. That's something I peeped about him from the giddy-up. On more than one occasion I had noticed these qualities in him, but Trish did not seem to care. To her it meant he really loved her, since he acted a fool if he thought even for a minute she was checking for another dude or vice versa.

They began to argue because Boss thought Trish was being too friendly with one of his boys. He grabbed her arm roughly and she snatched it away from him. They were so loud that they were causing a scene. It was a typical Trish and Boss fight, so nobody really paid that much attention. Usually they'd go back and forth a couple times and then the situation would be squashed. Trish would be right back on Boss's arm again like the little trophy wifey he made her out to be. So we all figured this argument would be no different—until Boss took it further than usual and backhanded Trish across the face. Trish just sat there in shock with her hand over the side of her face. She didn't move or say a word.

I, on the other hand, was on fire. "What is wrong with you? Don't put your hands on my sister! I don't care who you think you are!" I yelled as I got up in Boss's face.

"No! Summer, wait!" Trish screamed at me. "This ain't your business."

Now I was the one in shock. I couldn't believe Trish was snappin' on me in Boss's defense, which only infuriated me more. I guess Trish could see the smoke coming out of my ears because she tried to soothe things over by saying, "It's okay, Summer. I'm good."

What did she mean it was okay? Since when was it okay for a woman to let some man put his hands on her? I looked up to my sister far too much for her to become one of those women who allowed a man to do whatever he wanted to her whenever he wanted. The Flynt girls had a reputation to uphold, whether Trish knew it or not.

"It ain't okay, Trish!" I yelled. "It won't be too long before those slaps turn into punches," I warned.

"Chill," she said to me as if I were the one who had started all this mess. Boss just sat next to her with a stupid grin on his face; like he was proud that his baby had his back over mine.

I smacked my lips and shook my head. "You know what? Forget it. You be dumb if you want to." I headed upstairs. Someone turned the music up a notch louder and the festivities went on as if nothing had happened. I was steamed and just wanted to get out of there. I sat in Boss's living room without turning on any lights. The dark was calming, until Jus entered the room and turned on the lights.

"Turn 'em back off," I said in a low tone.

"You a'ight?" he asked as he clicked the light off and sat down beside me.

"She's just so stupid sometimes. I really don't like him," I replied.

"She's a big girl," he answered.

I couldn't see his facial expression in the dark, so I didn't know if he was being sarcastic.

"I just wanted to come and check on you," he said with a slight slur. "You got a hot top on you. You got a temper like a grown woman." He chuckled slightly.

"I am a grown woman," I stated playfully.

"Yeah, okay," he replied. This time, he laced his words with sarcasm.

An awkward silence fell over the room, and I could

feel the couch shifting underneath me as he came closer.

"Why you always playing games with me, Summer?" he asked in the most serious tone I'd heard him speak in to date.

"I'm not playing games with you, Jus." I paused for a moment, trying to choose my next words carefully. "I'm not feeling you like that." That was as careful as it was gonna get. "Is it that hard to believe that a girl can actually turn you down?" I asked. "You're cooler than I first expected you to be, I'll admit that, but how different can you be from the company you keep?" I continued without allowing him time to answer. "You hang with somebody I can't stand."

"I'm my own man," Jus stated.

"Whatever." I threw my hands up. I'd said all I needed to say. "Look, you feel like taking me home?" I asked.

"You ain't my girl, shorty. I'ma stop being your personal taxi. Every time I see you, you leave the party early and want me to take you to the crib," he complained.

"Just come on," I said, disregarding his noise as I stood up from the couch. I knew that he didn't mind taking me home, and if he did, I didn't care as long as he did what I wanted.

This time, Jus was in his car. He drove slowly toward downtown; not like that maniac speed-driving he did on his bike. When we arrived in front of my building, I reached for the door, but he popped the locks, trapping me inside. When I turned to face him so that I could dig into him about trying to hold me hostage in his ride, my lips met his without warning, and I fell into the trance of his kiss.

I know this might sound stupid, but believe it or not, this was my first kiss. I had lived for sixteen whole years and had never been kissed by a boy. I must admit, this was also the first time that I felt flutters in my stomach that seemed to trickle through every bone in my body. I caught myself shivering, as if a huge gust of wind had just whisked through the car. But it was anything but cold up in there as my temperature rose and I felt funny all over. I prayed to God that tiny specks of perspiration didn't start to cover my forehead, even though I felt like I was going to break out in a sweat at any moment.

The feeling that was taking over my body was indeed weird, but it was better than anything I'd ever felt before. The chemistry between Jus and me was insane, and I knew that I would never forget how that moment felt. My entire body was sensitive and tingly, but once I realized what I was doing, I pulled away.

"I–I got to go," I stuttered as I fumbled around for the button, unlocked the door, and got out of the car.

I didn't even say good-bye, thank you, or nothing. I walked quickly up the walkway, hoping Jus would just drive off and let me be. But that would have been too much like right.

"Summer!" he yelled after me.

I kept walking, pretending not to have heard him.

"Summer!" This time he called my name even louder. There was no way I could fake the funk, so I stopped in my tracks and turned around.

He had rolled the passenger window down and was leaning toward it. "I'll pick you up from school tomorrow. Okay?"

Thinking quick on my feet, I came up with something real fly to respond with. "So what are you now, my personal taxi?"

He dropped his head and chuckled. Then he looked up at me with this magnetizing smile and said, "Yeah, I guess so. Is that all right with you?"

I nodded and smiled then rushed into the building. I thought about his words back at Boss's place, when he said I wasn't his shorty and he wasn't my personal taxi driver. Well, since apparently he was game at being the latter of the two, I couldn't help but wonder about his thoughts on the former. But I was sure I'd find out soon enough.

The next day, school flew by, which was a first. I barely even talked to my friends all day, and when they talked to me, I half paid attention. I would just nod my head or say, "Mmm- hmm. Yeah." I wasn't trying to be funny, but I couldn't help it. All I kept thinking about was my first kiss.

I wondered if it mattered that it was Jus that I kissed. Would it had felt the same had it been any other boy, or did I have a connection with only Jus? I didn't know, but that kiss had made me look at Jus completely differently. It was always something making me change my opinion of him for the better.

When the final bell of the day rang, my girls and I walked side by side out of the building. Just as he had promised, Jus was sitting in the parking lot waiting for me to come out. His usual groupie broads were still doing everything under the sun to get his attention, but I didn't care. It was my lips he kissed, not theirs. And if I was lucky, and if he played his cards right, we'd have a repeat of last night.

I turned toward my crew and said, "I'll check y'all later. I'm riding with Jus."

They gave me an astonished look and Latina called out, "Chick, you better call me as soon as you get home! You ain't slick."

I laughed, then made my way over to Jus's car. I hopped in and threw the peace sign out of the window as Jus pulled off.

"What up, shorty?" he asked.

"You tell me," I responded.

Jus looked at me briefly and then focused back on the road. He turned up his speakers and nodded to Li'l Wayne's newest mix tape without responding. I just sat there with one hand on each knee, bobbing my head and tapping my fingers to the beat.

The next thing I knew, I felt a gentle touch on my hand, then looked down to see Jus intertwining his fingers with mine. A couple days ago, I would have put up a fight. But now things between us were definitely different.

He held my hand the entire way home, and just that little show of affection had me confused but excited. How had I ignored this boy for so long? Then again, maybe it was the fact that I had ignored him so much that attracted him to me. All the girls were doing everything they could to get him to spit game their way, but I was doing just the opposite.

A few minutes later, Jus pulled up to my building. I swear on everything that I didn't want to get out. I had to find something to say in order to stall. "Thanks for picking me up," I said.

"No problem, ma," he replied. He leaned over and pecked my lips. It was nowhere as intense as the first kiss, but I reveled in the moment anyway.

I put my hand on the door handle to get out, but then I halted. I was feeling way too confused about

Jus and me. I did not want to keep company with confusion for any longer than I had to, so I turned to Jus and asked, "What does this mean?"

"What does what mean?" he feigned dumb.

"The kiss," I told him. "The kisses."

"It means I like kissing you, and while I'm kissing you, I don't want none of those li'l Cass dudes you got sniffing behind you in the hallway kissing you, nah mean?"

Yes! I shouted in my head. I guess just like the song from *Making the Band,* we were now exclusive. I couldn't help but smile. Jus laughed, showing all his perfect teeth. Dang, that boy was so fine.

"Call me." I blushed—on purpose—and then gave him my phone number.

I watched as he pulled out his cell phone and stored the number. Now that my number was locked in his phone, my next step was to make sure I stayed locked in his mind because, although I didn't verbalize it to Jus, I liked kissing him too. And while I was kissing him, I didn't want none of those li'l Cass broads who were always sniffing behind him in the parking lot kissing him.

I was so high and excited, it felt like I floated into the building. I wasn't one hundred percent certain whether Jus and I were an official couple, since he hadn't just come straight out and said those words, but I knew that he was feeling me, and at that moment, it was all that mattered.

I waltzed to the apartment door as I sang the song "Exclusive." Nothing could mess up my buzz right about now, or so I thought.

I put my key in the lock, and before I could even get in and close the door behind me, I heard Trish say, "I've got to talk to you."

It was the first thing that Trish had said to me since last night over at Boss's spot. I'd heard her when she came in at the wee hours of the morning, but she just went straight to her room. Now all of a sudden the urgency in her voice caused me to stop dead in my tracks. I knew whatever it was she wanted to speak with me about was serious.

"What's going on?" I asked as I approached her. It was then that I saw the bruises around her neck and the black eye on her once perfect face. "What happened, Trish?" I know Boss had decked her one last night, but no way, no how had it done this much damage. He must have finished what he started after I left.

I touched her face. "Did Boss do this to you?" My blood boiled with rage. I knew from the first time I laid eyes on Boss that he was bad news. Trish deserved so much better than him. I couldn't understand why she liked him. "Tell me, Trish, did that fool do this to you?" I balled my fists. "Because if he did, I swear to—"

"Don't worry about my face, Summer. I'll be all right, but I need you to listen to me, okay?"

I nodded in understanding. "Okay, I'm listening. What could be more important than this?" I asked, motioning to her face to emphasize my point.

"Remember you saw me with all of that money in my room?" she asked.

I nodded. "Yeah. Your so-called savings."

She continued. "Well, it's not exactly my savings. It's more like savings from Boss's money." Trish tightened her lips as if she dreaded having to say the next words that came out of her mouth. "I've been taking money from Boss since I met him. Stashing a little bit for myself, a couple hundred at a time."

"Trish—"

"Wait." She cut me off again. "Let me finish."

Oh goodness, there's more? I thought as she continued.

"I lied to you when I said that I didn't know what was in those packages I was delivering for Boss." She swallowed. Hard. "Each time I made a drop-off, I was expected to bring back cash, and I always did. But I also always took a cut off the top."

I shook my head. That was Street Pharmacy 101:

You don't cut from the boss's cash. I'd been in a group home and not on the streets half my life, but even I knew that much. "You've been stealing from Boss? Is that why he messed your face all up?" I asked in a whisper as if someone else could hear me.

"No, he doesn't know. We got into it because I told him I wanted out. He has a big run that needs to be made tonight. He wants me to do it. When I told him I didn't want to, he slapped me around some . . . but it's no big deal," Trish stated.

"It is a big deal, Trish. Don't be stupid! This is serious," I yelled.

"Look, I already agreed to do it, Summer. It's too late for me to back out now, but I'm doing it for my own reasons." She walked in closer to me as if she were about to share some top secret information. "I have fifty thousand dollars underneath the floor in my bedroom. The money that I'm supposed to pick up tonight will make it one hundred thousand," Trish said.

I could not believe the words that had just come out of her mouth. "What?" I asked. "You sure you ain't taking some off the top of those drugs you delivering? Because you got to be on something to even think about doing something as stupid as that." I began to pace the floor. "You're lucky that Boss hasn't already found out that you been stealing from him. He might not have missed a couple hundred here and there, but fifty Gs, Trish. Are you crazy? You already have a lot of money. You need to just walk away," I urged.

"No, Summer. I mean, I'm going to walk away, but not until after I get what I want. As a matter of fact, I'm going to walk away tonight. We're going to walk away tonight."

I dreaded the answer, but I had to ask. "What do you mean, we're walking away?"

As matter-of-factly as she could put it, Trish answered, "We're leaving town tonight. I'm taking the other fifty thousand and starting a new life." She could see the disapproval of her little scheme written all over my face. "I'm doing this for us, Summer. We'll go down South or something. By the time Boss realizes what happened, we'll be long gone. So, I need you to pack your stuff and meet me at the Greyhound station at midnight. I want you to bring the fifty thousand dollars from my room. I'll have the other half when I meet you there," Trish stated.

I was stunned into silence. I couldn't believe that Trish was thinking of doing something like this. Here I was just getting used to my freedom and all, and now, with Boss surely to be on our tails, I'd feel like a prisoner all over again. I didn't want any part of this, and the look on my face said it all, so Trish continued to plead with me.

"Summer, I can't do this without you, sis."

As badly as I wanted to try to talk her out of this nonsense, I knew it would be in vain. Trish's mind was made up, and she was my big sis. I couldn't leave her hanging. "All right, Trish, I'll meet you," I relented.

A huge grin spread across her face. As if she had been sure al along that I'd go for her plan, she passed me a bus ticket and gave me a huge hug. "I love you, Summer. You're the only person that I can count on in this world. It's been just me and you for a while now. It's me and you against the world," she stated. "The world hasn't defeated us yet, and it never will, just as long as we stick together." She patted me on the shoulder. "Now, go get to packin'. We got a bus to catch." She winked with a smile before walking away.

Trish didn't seem fazed by the damage that Boss had done to her face. She went into her room, grabbed a suitcase full of her possessions, and headed toward the door. She was a determined woman.

She blew me a kiss and said, "Take a cab to the bus station and don't be late, sis. I love you."

"Love you," I responded.

Trish opened the door and started out. Right before she closed the door behind her, she stopped and turned around. "Midnight?" she asked, making sure I was on board.

I nodded along with a deep sigh. "Midnight," I confirmed.

Chapter Five

"Trish"

Tonight was the night it was all going down. It was payback time for Boss. I was tired of taking his crap, and I was even more tired of making these runs for him. He was a drug dealer, and even though I wasn't standing out on the corners slinging the stuff, by helping him pick up and drop off his shipments, I was no better than him. But tonight I was putting an end to all the madness. I had to do it, if not for me, then for my little sister.

I could see the disappointment in Summer's face when she figured out what it was that I really did for Boss. She was young and didn't understand the game, but like most players, I did it because I had to. I needed to make money so that I could take care of her. I had made her a promise that I would get her out of that group home, and I did what I had to do in order to make it happen.

I was her older sister, and my love for her could never go away. When the state released me from the group home at eighteen, I almost didn't want to leave. How could I leave my thirteen-year-old sister behind? I had tried to take her with me then, but the courts had a million and one reasons why I couldn't raise her on my own, and the most important one was money—or lack thereof. I really couldn't be mad at the system, because in all actuality, they were right. Like my mama used to say, I didn't have a pot to pee in or a window to throw it out of. Literally, all I had were the clothes on my back.

When I met Boss, I was surprised that he was even interested in me. I was working in the local Foot Locker when he came in with a group of other guys. He told me how pretty I was and how he had never met a girl with a smile as bright as mine. He charmed his way into my life, which I've now figured out was probably all part of his plan. He probably just never thought he would fall in love with his mule.

Of course, I was too blind to see his real agenda. I just thought he was a nice guy. Every day after our initial encounter he came back into the store and purchased a pair of shoes, and he always made sure that

I was the one who waited on him. At first I just thought he was ballin' out of control like that, but then my female intuition questioned whether it was really the shoes he was coming in for.

One day I asked him, "Do you really need all of these shoes?"

He smiled and answered, "Nah, I just need an excuse to stop in and see you. I don't want to seem like a stalker."

"Too late." I smiled.

"In that case, you might want to go ahead and file for a restraining order, because it's going to be impossible for me to keep away from you."

After that he had me. I always loved the quality of persistence in a person. He asked me out and I agreed. We went out several times, but I always made sure he picked me up from my job. Once someone of his caliber saw the jacked-up place where I was laying my head, I knew he'd have second thoughts. I felt like Jada Pinkett Smith in the movie *Set It Off* when she dated Blair Underwood's character; like Boss was out of my league, but I was going to play every inning for what it was worth.

Being with Boss made me forget about the ghetto, as he made sure to always show me a good time by introducing me to the finer things in life. He wined me and dined me at restaurants I never thought I would eat at. He took me to concerts and stage plays, always buying me a nice outfit to wear.

After a few dates, he wanted to get inside of my head. He wanted to know all about me, my life, and my family. By then I felt like I could share anything with this man. I told him my story about my mama and my sister; about how I was bound and determined to convince the courts that I could do just as fine a job of raising her as the home could.

One day after work, Boss took me out and we spent a wonderful evening by the water, just talking. Usually I was good about watching the clock so that I didn't miss the bus. See, for two months, I'd been having Boss drop me off at an apartment building where I wished I could live. From there, I'd catch the city bus home. But on this night, we'd fallen asleep talking and cuddling, and by the time we woke up, I knew the bus had stopped running.

I didn't have nearly enough money to cover the cab fare it would have taken for me to get from my fantasy apartment to my real dwelling, and I wasn't about to just straight-out ask Boss for cash. He did enough for me without me turning into some gold digging, begging chicken head. So I was forced to have him drop me off at my real spot. I told him it was a friend of mine's house and I was spending the night with her. That was when I first realized that Boss had a jealous streak.

Boss questioned me about my friend, how we'd met, and how long we had been friends. He asked why I hadn't mentioned any friends up until now. He was drilling me like those investigators on *First 48*. I folded and told him the truth. He let me know that I didn't have to be phony with him; that I could be real and that he cared about me, not where I lived.

That night Boss insisted on walking me to my door. When he saw the roach-infested apartment I was living in, he leased me a new apartment near the water. It just happened to be the apartment building I used to claim as mine and have him drop me off at. I swear no one could have written a better movie script or fairytale. I thought Boss was perfect—heaven sent. But all along, he was setting me up to work for him.

When he finally approached me about making runs, he told me that he had a way that I could make a lot of money. I was immediately interested. He said that all I had to do was drop off a package and pick up some money. It seemed simple enough, but I wasn't stupid. I knew he sold drugs. He could afford to buy shoes almost every day, which, I later learned, he would just give away to some of his corner boys. He took me to fancy places and drove a fancy car. Not once did he ever mention his place of business. And I never asked.

I was aware of the fact that I was getting involved in something illegal, but Boss had saved me. He had given me the start I needed to get Summer back. In addition to that, he had already done so much for me out of the kindness of his heart. How could I possibly tell him no? I was indebted to him, so I began to do the job.

He was right; the gig paid extremely well, and I used every dime to save up money and set up a future for Summer. It wasn't long, though, before I realized that Boss was paying me chump change compared to what he was making. That's when I began to chip off the top, little by little. He'd used me, so now I was using him.

I didn't just all of a sudden decide to bite the hand that fed me, but it hadn't taken me long to discover Boss's true personality. He was out for self, so I simply followed his lead. When I first met him, he played the role of a good guy. He was nice and sweet. I thought he would give me the world, but once he had me on board and I was trapped beneath his wing, Boss became controlling and violent. On the outside, I'd mastered the role of wifey, but on the inside, I couldn't stand him and I didn't feel bad about taking his money.

So far, I had managed to save $50,000, but tonight was different. It was the first run that I would make after Summer's release, and I wanted me and my sister to be straight. I wanted to leave Detroit and start over in a new city. In order to make that happen, I had to go for the gusto. I was taking Boss's entire pick-up money. By the time he realized what had happened, I would be in an entirely different state. Summer and I would be living well and carefree, and Boss would never be able to find me because I didn't plan on leaving behind any clues.

So now, here I stood in front of Boss's place for what would be the last time, to pick up and deliver the last package I ever would. I took a deep breath before walking up to his door and ringing the bell. He opened the door and let me in.

"Hey, babe," he said, kissing my bruised face.

I pulled away slightly. It was instinct. I'd told myself over and over not to act unusual, but his wet lips against my face just made me want to cringe.

"Everything all right?" He asked with a puzzled look on his face, concerned about my actions.

"Everything's good," I replied without an ounce of nervousness in my voice. "My face is just still a little tender, you know."

"Oh, baby," he said rubbing my face. "I'm so—"

"I know, Boss. You're sorry," I finished for him.

He pulled his hand away. "Yeah, I'm sorry."

I looked him dead in his eyes and said, "Yeah, Boss, me too." I shook the moment off. "Where's the package?"

"Hold up." Boss padded to his bedroom and then returned with the package. There was silence between us "You sure you all right?"

"I'm sure."

"I'll walk you out." Boss walked me to my car and placed the package in my trunk. I'd already climbed into the driver's seat. "I'll see you later then," he stated as he closed the trunk.

I rolled away, watching him watch me in my rearview mirror.

I drove the hour-long ride into Flint, Michigan. It was a smaller city, but just as grimy as Detroit, so I had to be careful and make sure everything went as planned. At this point, there was only one thing—or should I say one person—that could throw the plans off track: Summer. I mean, what if she was late getting to the Greyhound station or something? What if she decided to tell those friends of her good-bye? Or even worse, what if she talked to Jus?

All kinds of crazy thoughts went through my mind, and the more I thought about it, the more I wished I had just brought Summer with me and then caught a flight out of Flint to make our escape. But if something went wrong with the money exchange, I didn't want Summer to be involved. *No she's safer at home*, I concluded. She had her bus ticket. All she had to do now was meet me down at Greyhound and everything would be fine.

I'd managed to get my mind back on track, but I was still extremely nervous when I pulled up to the spot where I was supposed to meet Boss's associate. Something just didn't feel right, but I was too close to turn back now. Even if I wanted to turn back, it was too late as I saw the guy come out of the house toward my car. I popped the trunk and got out of the car to retrieve the package.

"Where's the money?" I asked when I noticed that his hands were empty.

"Boss called. He wants you to wait for him here," the dude responded.

I thought my heart was going to jump out of my chest right then and there. This was not a part of the plan. In all the time I had been making these runs, the routine had never changed. I knew that something was wrong. I began to back up toward the car door, but the guy sensed my need to flee and he grabbed my arm.

"I said Boss wants you to wait here," he whispered in my ear as he dragged me into the house.

I dropped my head to my chest. I wondered if Boss

had gone over to the apartment and caught Summer packing or something. Had he questioned her to the point where she gave in and told him our plan? The thought of what thugs and gangsters do to people once they bleed them for all the information they have ran through my mind as well. What if he'd killed my little sister? Even if he hadn't killed Summer, I knew that if he'd found out what I was up to, Boss wouldn't allow me to breathe another day.

A single tear slid down my face. One way or the other, I just knew that I'd never see my sister again. I only hoped that she would be okay.

Chapter Six

"Summer"

When Trish left, I began to second guess my decision of agreeing to meet her at the bus station and leave with her tonight. But it was too late to change my mind because the plan was already in motion. It was only four o'clock in the afternoon, so I had plenty of time to pack my things and gather my thoughts.

I had just gotten out of the group home and was starting to feel established, like I belonged somewhere and meant something to someone, and now I was being uprooted. I was leaving my friends and a possible boyfriend, but for my sister, I didn't have a choice. I'd follow her to the moon and back if she asked me to . . . even if it meant sacrificing my happiness.

I shook my head as I realized that my life just could not get stable no matter how hard I tried or how badly I wanted it to. Drama followed me everywhere. I looked around my new-but-soon-to-be-old room. Everything was so perfect that I wanted to call U-Haul and take everything with me. But I knew that I couldn't. Instead, I only packed the necessities, the small things.

All of my clothes, most of them with the tags still attached, were folded neatly into my luggage. Shoes, clothes, jewelry, and a picture of my friends was all that I was taking. Everything else would have to be left behind. I only hoped that I wasn't leaving behind a good life to step into a bad one. I had encountered enough bad times, and I felt that I deserved the current life that I was living. But somewhere deep inside, I knew that the storm was not over. It had only calmed for a while. I could see the dark clouds beginning to reform above my head.

Changing out of the clothes I had worn to school that day, I slipped into some Juicy Couture sweat pants and a white camisole to relax. If I was about to spend hours on a Greyhound bus, then I needed to be as comfortable as possible. I lay down on my bed and closed my eyes. I just wanted to be alone with my thoughts for a couple hours and get one last sleep in the only place that had felt like home—a place that I would soon leave behind.

I was aroused out of my slumber by hard knocks at the door. I sat up drowsily and looked at the clock on my nightstand. It was only nine o'clock, and I couldn't imagine who was at the door. My girls would have hit me up before just dropping by, so I knew it wasn't them. Trish wasn't supposed to come back to the apartment at all, and I wasn't due to meet up with her for another three hours.

Knock! Knock! Knock!

"Who the heck is this?" I made my body shake off the lazy sleep and I climbed out of bed. I wiped my eyelids and straightened my hair a little bit before heading toward the door.

"Okay, okay, I'm coming!" I shouted in irritation. I pulled open the door and was greeted by the police. A uniformed officer stood before me, while a plain-clothes detective stepped inside without being invited.

"Excuse me? Can I help you with something?" I asked as I placed a hand on my hip. I had no idea what they were doing here, but growing up in the system, I had acquired a big dislike for authority, including cops.

"Are your parents home?" the detective asked me

as he eyeballed the apartment, taking a couple steps into the living room area.

"My mother is dead," I stated matter-of-factly. "What is this about?" I was suspicious. The cop in uniform seemed uncomfortable as he stood there silently eyeing his partner.

I had no idea what these two clowns were up to. The first thought that entered my head was that Trish had gotten caught transporting for Boss and was locked up. My heart began to race at the idea of my sister being caught up in the system. If Trish was locked up, that meant that I would soon be heading back into the system myself. But then I realized that even if Trish did get caught and was in jail, at least I had the money to bail her out, so all would be well.

"How old are you?" the detective asked.

I frowned. I didn't know the purpose of his question, but for some reason, I felt the need to lie. "Eighteen. Now, what is this about?"

"Do you know this person?" he asked as he handed me a small plastic card. It was Trish's driver's license. I was sure then that he had arrested her and was coming to find out dirt on my sister.

"She's my sister. Where is she?"

Neither officer was quick to answer my question. They just looked at each other, then the uniformed cop dropped his head.

"There has been an accident," the detective started. "Your sister was found in an abandoned car. She's—"

I cut off the detective in hopes that his story was going to have an upside. "She's okay, though, right? I mean, abandoned car . . . was it stolen or something? Did you arrest her? I guarantee you that Trish didn't have anything to do with no stolen car. That was probably all her lousy boyfriend's doing. Because you know . . ." I talked ninety miles per hour as tears welled in my eyes. I didn't know how long the officers were going to let me go on and on with this small ray of hope I had of Trish being able to walk through that door again. But as the detective started shaking his head in response to everything I was saying, I knew the ending of his story was much different than the one I was telling.

The detective, in order to cut me off, finally walked over and put his hand on my shoulder. "Miss, I'm sorry, but your sister was shot," he said solemnly. "She's—"

"She's at the hospital," I interrupted once again. Now the tears had escaped my eyes and were rolling down my cheeks. "But she's going to be okay, right?" I began to pace back and forth as I looked for my purse and keys. "What hospital is she at so I can go check on her? Just let me get my purse and keys and—"

The detective finally got a word in edgewise. "She's dead. I'm sorry, Miss, but your sister is dead."

I stopped pacing. "What?" I asked. "No, not Trish. Not my sister. There has to be some mistake. No. No!" I screamed. I looked over at the uniformed officer who hadn't spoken much. I gave him a look, as if pleading for him to tell me that his partner here was lying; that Trish was alive and well. But there was no such luck.

The uniformed officer simply removed his hat and said, "I'm sorry, Miss."

The detective cleared his throat and lowered his head. "She was dead on our arrival. We need a family member to come down to our examiner's office to identify the body."

Everything around me went blank and my heart felt as if it had exploded. I think I was numb to the fact that Trish was gone. My mind couldn't comprehend what the man was telling me. I had just seen Trish a couple hours ago. How could she be dead? It wasn't possible . . . was it? I grabbed a jacket from the closet and slipped on a pair of sneakers.

"I want to see my sister," I said almost inaudibly. *It's probably not even her,* I thought, still not giving up the last ounce of hope I had in me. I refused to believe it until I saw it.

I followed the police to their car and was escorted to the city morgue. Just stepping inside of the building frightened me. The bright lights seemed to illuminate a stale bluish haze, and the floor echoed beneath my feet. It was eerie. Both officers kept looking back at me, as if I would break at any moment, but I still didn't believe them. I still didn't believe my Trish was dead. It was too unreal. People don't just die without warning. God wouldn't do this to me again. He wouldn't take my sister too.

"It can't be her," I whispered to myself.

I was led into a room filled with large drawers lined all up and down the walls. Some were open, with long steel slabs pulled out. I assumed it was where the bodies were stored. There was one body on top of a metal table in the middle of the room. A stark white sheet hid the identity, and I held my breath in anticipation as I approached.

"Show her," the detective instructed the forensic examiner. The Latina woman pulled back the sheet, and my hand flew to my mouth to stifle my cries.

"Oh my God! No," I cried out. The tears blinded me and the contents of my stomach came up involuntarily. "Aghh," I wailed, holding my stomach. I ran out of the room and tried to escape the harsh reality of the situation.

"Wait . . . hey, hold up!" the detective yelled.

I ran as fast as I could, ignoring his calls, but my legs gave out on me and I fell to my knees with my face in my hands as my soul spilled out onto the cold, hard floor.

The detective kneeled by my side and removed a handkerchief from his jacket pocket. "I'm sorry, and I know this is a horrible time, but I need to ask you some questions regarding your sister's murder."

I nodded my head and he helped me rise from the floor. My face was stained with tears, but I controlled my sobs as I walked to the nearest bench with my head hanging low.

"What's your name?" he asked me after pulling out a pad and pencil.

"Summer," I replied. "Summer Flynt."

"Summer, do you know anyone who would want to harm your sister?" he asked. "She had bruises and scratches on her face and neck. Did she have a fight with someone?"

I was too distraught to answer any questions. Every time I opened my mouth to speak, nothing but air came out. I knew what had led to Trish's death. Her involvement with Boss had cost her her life. I was not stupid; I figured that Boss had found out that Trish was stealing from him and that this last run was nothing but a setup on his part.

"We had plans. We were supposed to leave tonight. We were moving to Atlanta," I said. I was hysterical. I could not help it. After waiting for so long to be reunited with my family, Trish was taken away from me in the blink of an eye.

The detective must have noticed that I was in no state to talk. He sighed and pulled out a card.

"Listen, here is my contact information. Go home and get some rest. Get yourself together a bit. I really am very sorry about your loss. Call me when you're up to answering a few questions," he said. "I'll have an officer take you back home."

I nodded and hugged myself tightly. I had goose bumps all over my body. I felt like my entire body was freezing, and I couldn't stop the uncontrollable shaking that had taken over my limbs.

I was escorted to a police car and driven back to the apartment. I got out without thanking the officer. What did I have to thank him for? I know everyone says that you should never shoot the messenger, but they were the only ones I had to blame. I couldn't take my pain out on anyone else, so for the time being, the police and I could not coexist.

I began to walk into my building, but stopped when I saw two known members of Boss's entourage coming out.

What are they doing here? I watched them get into their car and sit for a couple minutes. It was then that I realized that they weren't leaving. *Boss killed Trish. He must have found out about her stealing from him, and now he's looking for the rest of his money,* I thought frantically as I crouched behind a Dumpster at the rear of the parking lot. I knew it was likely that they were after me too. Boss probably thought that I knew where his money was.

I couldn't let him find me. I decided to wait until his crew left.

I had been in such a rush to join the detectives that I had forgotten to grab my coat. The November wind cut through my jean jacket like a knife as I crouched behind the Dumpster, waiting impatiently. I was freezing and afraid. I was alone. At the hands of Boss, a man I had never liked, Trish had met her end. I didn't want to meet mine, too, so I knew that I had to disappear. Both the money and I had to disappear.

There was no way I could give Boss his money. Without Trish, I was on my own. I knew the state would try to take me back into custody until I turned eighteen, and I refused to have my freedom taken away. Besides, Trish shed blood over that money. It belonged to me now. Boss took my sister; the money was the least he owed me.

My fingertips turned blue and my thighs burned at the bite of the wind. I crouched down low to keep warm and blew my breath into my hands for heat. I hoped that Boss's boys would leave soon so that I could go inside, get the money, and jet.

I had no clue that they would be so relentless. They waited all night and even into the morning. It wasn't until one of the maintenance workers came to empty the building's trash into the Dumpster that I caught a break. By that time, I was shivering so badly that I could barely stand.

"Excuse me, ma'am, can you please help me?" I asked the female worker, my teeth chattering so badly that I could barely get the words out.

"Oh goodness!" the lady yelled.

"Shh!" I warned. I looked over to the car to make sure her outcry hadn't caught their attention. "Listen, I need your help."

"I'm sorry, I don't have any money," she replied. "I'm just emptying the trash."

"Wait, please! I don't want any money. I'm not homeless. I live in the building you are cleaning. My sister was killed last night, and I think the people who killed her are after me. You see that black car over there?" I asked as I pointed toward the other end of

the lot. I had her full attention, so I spoke quickly before she decided to write me off. "Those men are
watching the building, waiting for me to show up. I
need to get inside there and grab some things from
my apartment," I pleaded.

"No," the lady stated. "I don't want any part of
this."

"Please!" I begged. "All you have to do is let me
hop inside your garbage bin and roll me back inside.
When I'm done, just roll me back out. I'll even pay
you."

"How much?" the lady asked skeptically.

"A hundred dollars," I said.

She wheeled the large trash can behind the Dumpster and I hopped inside. She put the top over it, and
I felt her begin to move.

My plan worked like clockwork. She wheeled me
all the way to my front door, which was slightly ajar. I
climbed out and opened the door all the way to find
that the place was in shambles. Couch cushions had
been sliced to shreds, closets and cabinets had been
cleared. It was then that my suspicions were confirmed. Boss had definitely killed Trish, and now he
was coming for me.

I rushed into Trish's room. I knew that they hadn't
found the money because they wouldn't have still
been waiting for me. I pulled up the floor tiles and

pulled up the black duffel bag. The cleaning lady looked at me suspiciously.

"Just wait a second," I whispered. "I have to get one more thing." I went into the kitchen and searched through the drawers. I wanted to have something of my sister's. I was trying to find the digital camera that Trish had used to take our picture the night of my birthday. I found it and quickly located the digital picture of me and Trish. We both looked so happy and carefree. I was grateful to have a memento of Trish. It was a picture that I would keep forever.

"Now roll me back out to the Dumpster. I'll pay you when I get back outside," I promised. She did as she was told. I gave her two hundred-dollar bills and then I ran as fast as I could in the opposite direction of the car full of henchmen.

My lungs burned as I went as far as my legs would take me. Cabs were not a dime a dozen in Detroit like they were in other major cities. I mean we had them, but I would have to call one, then wait for it to arrive, and I definitely was not trying to sit still for too long. I had to keep it moving and come up with a plan.

I knew that I looked a mess. I couldn't take anything with me. The suitcase that I had packed was useless because I couldn't sneak it out of the apartment with me. All I had were the clothes on my back and a duffel bag full of stolen money.

My body was exhausted, and I still couldn't shake the image of Trish from my mind. I needed to clear my head, but that would mean that I had to find a place to rest. I couldn't get a hotel room. I wasn't old enough to rent one on my own.

I kept my face turned toward the buildings as I walked. I didn't want anyone to recognize me, or Boss to ride by and find me.

The freezing Michigan air nipped at me like a small dog. I was so cold that my eyes had begun to produce involuntary tears. As they rolled down my face, the wind froze them instantly, only making it more painful for me to keep moving. Every few seconds, I ducked into a store to warm up. I rubbed my hands together furiously, trying to create heat from the friction. I knew that I would never survive on the streets of Detroit this time of year. The winter hawk was too vicious. I would need to find heated shelter if I wanted to make it through the night.

I decided to call one of my friends. I didn't want to bring them into my drama, but at the moment, I didn't have much of a choice. After locating a pay phone, I dialed Mya's cell phone number, collect. Luckily, she accepted the charges.

"Why are you calling me collect?" She asked.

"Mya, Trish is dead!" I cried out. "I need your help.

I need a place to crash for a couple days. Please come and get me."

"Oh my God! Where are you?" She asked. Her voice was filled with worry, and at that moment, I was glad that I had decided to make friends. Right now, they were my ace in the hole; the only people in the world who I could turn to.

"I'm on Jefferson by the arena," I explained as I looked around nervously. "Please hurry, Mya, and don't tell Latina. You know she will have my business all over town by the time you get here."

"I'm on my way," Mya assured.

I disconnected the call, ducked into a parking structure to shield myself from sight, and waited for Mya to arrive. I hoped that she hurried. I didn't know how much longer I could last like this.

Thirty minutes later, I saw Mya's car approaching. I began to step onto the street, but then I saw that she had a guy riding with her. My heart skipped a beat when I realized I had seen his face before at one of Boss's parties.

Why is he riding with her? I asked. *Are my friends in trouble because of me?* I looked at Mya's face and tried to find a sense of fear, but there was none. She didn't look like she was afraid of the guy beside her. In fact, she was talking to him calmly. I didn't know what they were talking about. I wasn't too great at lip reading, but one thing was for sure: the fact that the two of them were together sent up red warning flags in my head. After they passed by, I ran to the same pay phone and dialed Mya's number collect again.

"Hey, girl, where are you?" She asked calmly.

"Is everything okay?" I asked.

"Yeah, I'm just looking for you. I'm by the arena now," Mya responded, sounding carefree.

"Did you tell anyone? Is Tara with you?" I asked. I wanted to give her a chance to explain why she was riding with a passenger. *What is he doing with you?* I thought.

"No, you told me to keep it on the low, so I did," Mya responded. "I came alone." Mya told a bold-faced lie. I couldn't believe she would do something like that to me. I smelled a setup, but I couldn't understand why she would sell me out to Boss's crew. I hung up the phone on her.

I was about to run when I felt a hand cover my mouth and drag me away. Someone had found me.

I wasn't going down without a fight. I screamed and kicked, and then I bit down into my attacker's hand and ran without looking back. I wasn't going to give him a chance to catch up to me.

I darted back into the parking garage, but I was cut off by the screech of tires as a car came to a sharp stop directly in front of me. Jus hopped out of the car.

"Get in the car!" He yelled as he shook his bleeding hand.

"No!" I looked from left to right for a place to run. I started to take off, but I heard another car approaching.

"Trust me and get in now!" He yelled.

I didn't know what to do, but I definitely did not want Mya and Boss's other worker finding me. I had to put my trust in Jus. I got in, and so did he.

"Get in the back seat and lie down," he whispered as he checked his rearview. I did what I was told.

My adrenaline was on high and my fear was at its all-time peak. The warmth in his car began to chip away at my freezing exterior. I shook violently as I hid out in his backseat, lying as low on the floor as I could possibly get. I didn't know what was going to happen next. Jus could easily drive me directly to Boss, but for some reason, I didn't think that he would.

I heard a car approaching, and Jus rolled down his window.

"Yo, did you see her, fam?" I heard a guy ask.

"Nah, I just whipped through here and I can't find her anywhere," Jus replied coolly. He lied so well that I almost believed him myself.

Why is he helping me? He probably wants the money for himself.

"She just called me. She has to be around here somewhere," I heard Mya say. If I wasn't so afraid, I would have gotten out of the car and beat the braids off of her. She was supposed to be my girl, but here she was being a traitor.

How could she do this to me? I told her that my sister was just killed. She's supposed to be my friend. It was at that moment that I realized that friendships weren't built the way they used to be. No one had any loyalty anymore, and every man or woman was always out for self. Look at Mya . . . she was willing to turn me in. Look at Jus . . . he was going against Boss to help me. Even though his betrayal against Boss benefited me, I still knew that friendships could not be trusted.

"A'ight, look, I'm about to hit the block for a minute. Call Boss and let him know she got away, but we'll find her eventually," Jus instructed. "And keep a look out for her. Spin around here a few more times to make sure she's not here before you leave," he instructed.

"All right then, man," the guy said. "Peace."

Jus pulled away. "Stay down," he said, barely moving his lips when he spoke.

"Why would Mya do this to me?" I asked aloud. I

did not expect him to answer the question. I was really talking to myself.

"You can't trust anybody, Summer. Boss put a twenty-five thousand–dollar contract on your head. That's a lot of money, and I know a lot of people who are trying to get their hands on that. Whatever it is that you and your sister took from him, he wants it back with interest," Jus said.

"Please just let me go!" I pleaded.

"I'm not going to hurt you, Summer. I don't need the bounty. Just stay down and be quiet until we get to my spot," he said. I followed his instructions. I needed all the help I could get, at least until I figured out how I was going to get myself out of the mess that Trish had made.

When we arrived, Jus ushered me out of the car quickly, and instead of waiting for the elevator in his building, we took the stairs to the fifth floor. He was silent, and I still wondered if he would turn me in for the money. I didn't want to trust someone who was so closely connected to my sister's murderer, but at that point, I really didn't have a choice. I couldn't be picky about who helped me out or how they did it. I had to take what I could get.

Jus's apartment was immaculate for a boy his age. At only nineteen, he seemed to have himself together.

I stood nervously at the doorway, not knowing what to expect.

"Have a seat," he stated as he closed all of the blinds in the living room. "You're shaking," he observed. He went into one of the bedrooms and came back with a blanket. He wrapped it around me and said, "This should warm you up. You hungry?"

I nodded and he went into the kitchen. He pulled out a frozen pizza and put it into the oven while I stood in a daze, thinking about how quickly my life had gone from sugar to s-h-i—you know the rest. I don't have to spell it out.

"Why is this happening to me?" I asked. My voice trembled and I broke down as I collapsed into the cushions of his sectional.

"What did your sister take?" Jus asked.

I opened the duffel bag and revealed the money. "Are you going to give me up to Boss?" I asked.

"Come here." He motioned me over to him.

I stood, and when I was within arm's reach, it was instinctive for me to fall into his embrace. I cried without shame. For some reason, I felt safe in his arms.

"Shh!" He soothed. "I'm sorry about your sister," he said, showing me sympathy. I knew he felt sorry for me.

It felt good to be held. It gave me a small sense of

security, and I was grateful for the compassion that he showed. He didn't ask too many questions. I suppose it was because he already knew the details. He gave me time to think and to clear my head, and it was much needed and appreciated.

Mya had turned on me, so I was sure that all of my other girls also knew about the bounty. Even if they didn't know and offered me a place to lay my head, I would feel bad about bringing danger to their doorstep, so I knew I was all I had. Beyoncé said it best: Me, myself, and I was all I had in the end.

Jus pulled the food from the oven and I sat on one of the bar stools as he placed a plate of pizza in front of me.

"She was the only person I had," I whispered. "What am I going to do?" I just sat there shaking my head.

"Give Boss back his money," Jus said as he sat down beside me. He made it sound so simple, but my life was much more complicated than average.

"No! I need that money. Trish may have been wrong for taking it in the first place, but she died for it." My eyes began to tear up. "He didn't have to kill her. I'm keeping that money." My tone was adamant. "I'm only sixteen. If the state catches me, then I get shipped to some group home. I need that money to survive until I turn eighteen. He owes me that much," I yelled.

"I hear you, Summer, but it's a respect thing with Boss. He will kill you, and he'd kill me if he knew you were here right now," Jus said.

"Then I need to get to him first," I said.

"What are you going to do, Summer? Huh? You gon' kill him?" Jus asked, trying to talk some sense into me. It wasn't working, though. I was determined. I wanted to get revenge for Trish.

"I don't know, maybe!" I yelled defensively.

Jus sighed in frustration and I kept on yelling. "Well, what do you want me to do?"

"I don't have the answer to that question," Jus replied.

I thought of Trish lying there lifelessly and I closed my eyes. Tears warmed my face and I felt his arms embrace me. "I just want to help you," he comforted. "But we have to do this the right way."

"He has to go to jail," I concluded. "It's the only way that I'm going to be able to keep this money and walk around this city without watching over my shoulders every other second. I have to prove that he killed Trish."

"I'm not a snitch, Summer," Jus said as he released me.

"Jus! It's not about that stupid street code. My sister is dead! What if it were your sister or brother or mother or whoever that he murdered over some money? And you saw how he treated Trish when she was alive. He has to pay for this. In your world, snitches get stitches, but in the real world where a life is really worth something, murderers get jail time."

"I don't know if I'm with this," Jus admitted as he exhaled loudly. "How did I get myself into this?"

The fact that he couldn't see where I was coming from only infuriated me more. "You know what? It's cool. I don't need your help. Just when I was beginning to think that you were different, you showed me who you really are," I said.

"Summer, don't . . ."

Jus tried to grab my arm, but I snatched it away as I backed up. "Don't touch me! You are no better than him! As a matter of fact, you're worse because you sit back and do nothing while he hurts people. Just stay away from me."

I opened the front door and ran with the bag of money hanging off of my arm. I couldn't count on Jus and I couldn't trust him. Anyone who was associated with Boss was my enemy.

I felt stupid because I had actually liked Jus, and I wanted badly for him to like me. Now I was out for myself, and I had to hit the block in order to survive. But the first thing I had to get was a coat or else Boss wouldn't have to kill me; I'd die from the cold.

I stopped in the first clothing store that I came across and grabbed a fifty-dollar jacket, then went to the nearest hotel. The clerk behind the desk was a young blond woman.

"Can I help you?" she asked.

"Yes, I need a room," I said, trying to appear older than I actually was.

The girl looked at me skeptically. "You got an ID?" She asked.

"Oh yeah, here it is." I reached into the bag and pulled out a hundred-dollar bill. She picked up the money and eyed me suspiciously. "I need a room," I repeated, this time more sternly.

"Okay," she said. She took my information, which was bogus, because I wasn't staying in the hotel under my real name, and then she handed me a key card to a room on the second floor.

I was paranoid. Every person that looked my way, I instantly suspected they worked for Boss.

I was sleep deprived and emotional. I needed to get myself together so that I could have a clear head. I went into my room and peeled out of my clothes. The first thing I did was take a shower. I was so cautious that I propped a chair up against the bathroom door so that no one could get in unless I moved it. I wasn't taking the chance of Boss getting to me before I got to him.

When I turned on the shower, the salt from my tears mixed with the flow of fresh water, and I felt a sense of relief, as if I could wash away all of the bad memories.

I should have talked Trish out of leaving last night. I should have made her listen to me when I told her Boss was bad news.

I had so many regrets that they were weighing me down. I felt guilty, and although deep inside I knew that I had nothing to do with Trish's death, I still felt like it was my fault. I now held the same amount of heartache and remorse about Trish as I did for my mother. I should have been there for both of them; I had let them down. I wallowed in my sorrows. I was so lost in my thoughts that even after the water ran cold, I still stood there.

Eventually I stepped out of the tub and realized that I needed some clothes. The clothes that I had were filthy from being outside all night. Going out to the mall or going shopping would have been too risky. I needed to lay low for a while and move in silence so that I would surprise Boss instead of him surprising me. I was already at a big disadvantage. It was me against the world, but by knowing where to find him and keeping my location a mystery, I had leveled the playing field.

No, I can't go to the mall, I concluded. I definitely couldn't count on Mya to bring me more clothes. She had already tried to get me caught up for the money. *I could call Latina, but she talks too much. The entire city will know how and where to find me. My only option is Tara.* I didn't know if Tara would try to play me dirty the same way that her sister had, but she was the only one I was willing to take a chance on.

I picked up the hotel phone and made sure that I dialed *67 before dialing Tara's cell phone. Fortunately, she answered on the first ring.

"Hello?"

"Tara, it's Summer. Whatever you do, do *not* tell Mya I'm on the phone," I blurted out before she could bust me out.

"Mya's not home. What's wrong? You and Mya got into it or something?" She asked.

"You haven't heard yet?" I asked.

"Heard what?"

"Boss shot Trish last night and now he's after me. He put a contract out in the streets for me, Tara . . . I really need your help, but I need to know I can trust you."

"Of course you can trust me, Summer. We're girls," she assured.

"Are you sure about that?" I asked. "Your sister has already tried to lead one of Boss's workers to me. She tried to get me caught up earlier to get the reward money that Boss is promising for whoever catches me."

"I wouldn't do that to you. You are one of the few friends I have that likes me for me. Everybody else only wants to be around me to get closer to Mya. She was wrong, Summer. You don't have to worry about me. What do you need me to do?" She asked.

I hesitated before answering. I didn't want to tell her where I was, but she was my only option and I needed something to wear. "Can you bring me some clothes? About a week's worth. I'm at the Holiday Inn up the street from Northland," I said. "Room one twenty-one."

"Mya has our car, but I'll borrow my mom's whip and be there in a few," she promised.

"Okay. Thanks."

"Hey, Summer?"

"Yeah?"

"I'm so sorry about Trish. That's real messed up what Boss did to her. He is going get his one day. Karma will come back to him in time."

"Maybe some time soon," I said aloud. I hung up the phone.

I wasn't dumb. I gave Tara the wrong room number. I sent her to the room directly underneath me so that I could see if she was trying to set me up. I wouldn't get caught slipping like I had the first time. This time, I would be prepared. I would have an escape route planned if I smelled anything funny.

I knew it would take Tara about twenty minutes to get to the hotel. I put on my dirty clothes and waited in the room nervously for about fifteen minutes, and when I thought she was near, I made my way to the lobby. I sat in one of the patron chairs and picked up the free newspaper that was on the table. I opened the paper wide so that I could not be seen.

Not even five minutes later, Tara came in. I heard her as she asked the receptionist where room 121 was. I peeked around the paper and saw that she was alone. After she had walked down the hallway, I ran to the entrance and peeked outside to make sure no one was waiting for her out there. Once I was satisfied, I walked down to 121, where Tara stood outside the door, knocking.

"Hey, that's not my room," I said as I approached her.

She turned around and walked over to me. She gave me a hug and looked at me sadly. "Isn't this the one you told me?" She asked as she handed me a bag of clothes.

"Yeah, I needed to make sure you were alone," I admitted.

"Mya really turned on you?" She asked in disbelief.

"The world turned on me," I whispered as I made my way to the staircase, Tara following closely behind.

We went into my real room and I spilled the content of the bag on the bed. Tara had put clothes, undergarments, pajamas, a cell phone, and even a couple books inside. *"Diary of a Street Diva,"* I said aloud as I read one of the titles. "I don't think I'll need the books, but thank you anyway for being a good friend." I hugged her tightly. I appreciated the gesture.

I slipped into some clean pajamas and then sat down on the bed. She was a size smaller than me, but I could still fit her clothes, I just filled them out a lot better than she did.

"Are you okay?" Tara asked.

"Not really, but I will be once I get some things in order," I responded.

"What are you going to do?"

"Do what I always do—survive. I'm used to it. The only thing that hurts is the fact that I knew Boss was a bad guy. I just felt it. From the first time I met him, I didn't like him. There was something about him that just did not sit right with me. Now Trish is dead. I miss her."

I quickly wiped the tears from my eyes. I was tired of crying. It wasn't getting me anywhere. By being a crybaby, I was giving Boss power over me, and I had vowed the day I came to live with Trish that no one would have ever have power over me again. I controlled my world and everything in it. It was time for me to start acting like it. I couldn't think like a child anymore or even a carefree teen, because for some reason, God put me on the fast track from the very beginning. I grew up fast . . . too fast. Nothing about my life was carefree. I had the stresses of a grown woman, so it was time for me to become one. Technically, and by law, I was underage, but I considered myself a woman.

"Everybody knows playing with Boss is like playing with fire, Summer. Trish made some bad decisions, but it's not on you. Just be careful, okay? I don't want anything to happen to you."

Tara was a good friend. In fact, I think she was my best friend. I had always thought that Mya and I were the closest of our crew, even Latina and I were cool, but before tonight, Tara and I were only associated because we were in the same clique. I always viewed her as extra, but I now realized that she was the realest one out of the group.

"Don't worry about me, T. Nothing is going to happen to me. You're a really good friend, and if I never told you before, I love you, girl. You're my best friend, and really the only person I trust," I admitted.

"I love you too, girl. I better get out of here. Don't worry about anybody coming here. I won't tell anybody that I've even heard from you. I'll act like I don't know a thing," she assured.

I walked her to the door and said good-bye. I hid the money in the hotel room safe and then folded my dirty clothes. As I picked up my old jeans, a card fell from the pocket. I picked it up.

Detective Myerss, I thought, *I'm going to do your job for you and lead you straight to my sister's killer.*

I kept the light on because something about turning it out made my skin crawl. I wasn't afraid of the dark or anything, but until I felt safe, I needed to see what was around me at all times. I couldn't underestimate Boss. Trish had done that, and now she was gone. I was young, but determined to win. I was going to seek justice for my sister. I had never done it for Mama because I was too young to really understand exactly what had gone down, but this was my chance for redemption.

I flipped the business card in my hand nervously as I decided how I would approach Detective Myerss. I had to be careful or he would find out my real age and try to place me back under the watchful eye of the state. All I really had now was my independence. If that was taken away, then I had nothing. I was sure that I could take care of myself. Trish had left me with a lot of money. Once Boss was behind bars, I could live my life in peace.

I picked up the phone and dialed the detective's number. It was game time.

Chapter Seven

"Tara"

Iwas afraid for Summer. She didn't look too good, and I knew she had nowhere and no one to turn to. I felt as if I should have helped her in some other kind of way besides just taking her a bag of clothes. But what could I do? And my sister Mya . . . I couldn't believe she would even stoop so low. She's done some messed up things in the past, but this took the cake. Summer was supposed to be our girl, and even though we just met her a couple months ago, in the short time we had known her, she had never done anything to deserve what Mya did to her.

With Trish dead, Summer had no one here in Michigan to have her back. Now, she'd probably even have to go back living with her parents in Atlanta. I didn't know where her parent were at a time like this and why they weren't here for her when their daughter needed them most. Maybe they were just uncaring people. I don't know. Summer never talked about them, so I just figured they weren't close. But then again, I had a feeling that some of the great stories Summer told us about growing up down South were lies. For all I know, there were no parents back in Atlanta. If Summer did have parents, wouldn't they be here by now?

No, I was certain that Summer had lied to us, but I was sure that she had her reasons for doing so.

I couldn't believe that the exact same crowd that we used to love to hang around was now gunning for Summer. Boss was 23, and his crew of young hustlers ranged from 18 to 24. He had followers all over the city, so there was no telling who was after Summer.

I had been so dumb to think that hanging around people like Boss was cool. Any one of us could have easily ended up like Trish, dead and forgotten, all because we were trying to be down with the wrong crowd.

I prayed for a different ending for Summer. She deserved better. I didn't know what she had been through, but Summer was much more seasoned than any of us. She had the mentality of a young girl who had seen grown-woman things, so I knew that she could hold her own. I only hoped that she was a match for the kingpin that she was going up against. The type of people who worked underneath Boss had nothing to lose, so it was nothing for them to go all out to try to find her.

Money had the power to turn best friends against each other, so I knew that Summer was definitely in trouble. One thing was for sure, though, I wouldn't tell anybody that I had seen her. I was not going to feed her to the sharks like Mya had done. She was cold for that one, and although she was my sister, her actions had been fake. I knew all along that Mya had silently envied Summer; I just never thought she would stoop so low or go so far to get rid of her competition.

When I pulled up to the house, I noticed that Mya had returned home. I sighed, wishing that I didn't have to deal with her. I wanted to confront her about what she had done to Summer, but doing so would be admitting that I had been in touch with Summer, and I couldn't put my girl at risk like that.

I walked into the house and my mama immediately put me on blast.

"How's your friend?" She asked.

"What friend?" Mya automatically countered. She looked at me suspiciously. It was almost like she could see right through me.

"She's fine," I said as I handed my mother her car keys. "Thanks, Ma. I appreciate it." I kissed my mother on her cheek and headed directly upstairs toward my room. Mya was hot on my trail.

"Tara, did you see Summer?" She asked, stopping me at the top of the steps.

"No, why?" I replied, keeping it cool.

"Isn't that the friend you went to go see?" Mya was all too anxious for answers. I could tell by the anticipation in her voice.

"I didn't really go see a friend. I went for a drive so that I could smoke some weed without Ma finding out," I lied. I knew my story was sketchy because I didn't even smoke. I had tried it once only because Mya had pressured me to, but other than that, I was drug free.

Mya cut her eyes at me. I knew she didn't believe me, but whatever. That was my story and I was sticking to it.

"Oh, well, if you do hear from Summer, let me know."

"I will," I said as I took a couple of steps toward my room. I stopped and faced Mya. "Why are you looking for her so tough? You haven't talked to her today? Y'all usually speak every day," I said slickly.

"Nobody has heard from Summer. You didn't hear

about Trish?" she asked, seeming to forget her suspicions of my whereabouts.

"Nah, what about her?" I played dumb. Mya loved to be the one with the 411. She felt like she had the upper hand if she knew about stuff first. But usually it was Latina who beat her to the punch.

"Boss killed Trish last night for stealing from him. Now Summer is on the run with Boss's money and he has the whole hood looking for her. I need to warn her because whoever finds her first gets twenty-five thousand dollars," Mya said excitedly.

"I'd turn her in for all that money," I said. I wanted to throw out the bait to test Mya. I needed to know if Summer's suspicions were correct.

A devilish grin crossed my sister's face and she leaned in and whispered, "I know. That's why it's important for us to find her first. I don't know about you, but I could use that money."

I put on a fake smile and replied, "In that case, I'll let you know if I hear from her."

I walked into my room and closed the door behind me. I slid my back down the door and sighed deeply. *Good Luck, Summer. You're going to need it. With friends like my sister, who needs enemies?*

Chapter Eight

"Jus"

I felt bad for Summer. I knew that she was all alone, and I felt stupid for letting her leave the way she did.

I was feeling Summer. At sixteen, she was three years younger than me, but there was something about that girl that I loved. From the very first time I met her, I knew that she was different from every other girl on the block. I wanted to be there for her.

I basically saved her life in that parking garage, but what she was asking me to do now was against the code. She wanted me to snitch on Boss. It wasn't my loyalty that was stopping me from doing it, because even I had to admit that Boss was a cold and cruel individual. I had personally witnessed Boss put fear in the hearts of men in their thirties, so honestly, Trish didn't stand a chance. Why she would even think of stealing from Boss was beyond me. The girl had to have a death wish.

On the real, I had never been too fond of Trish. She was cool and all, but to me she didn't stand out. She was just like all the other girls in Detroit. She was a girl with an addiction to material possessions, and in order to live a certain lifestyle, she linked up with Boss. If she really knew how crazy Boss was, she would have run the other way, but girls always overlooked the flaws of men with money.

Trish was infatuated with the money, not the man, and she allowed him to disrespect her as long as he kept money in her pocket. I actually expected Summer to be exactly like her sister, but I was pleasantly surprised when she proved me wrong.

Summer looked like a young knock-off of her sister. They were both drop dead gorgeous, but Summer's personality was drastically different from Trish's. She seemed unimpressed by Boss's lifestyle, and no matter how hard I tried to come at her, she never fully let me in. I always felt like there was this wall she had up. That's probably why I liked her so much, because of the chase. No boy wants a girl that gives herself away easily or who can be bought. Summer was neither. It took me four whole months just to get a kiss out of her. She was headstrong and smart. Young, fly, and flashy, I knew that she had to be my girl. I knew eventually I could chisel my way through that wall.

Everything was on track until Trish ended up dead. Now Summer wanted me to go against everything that I stood for to talk to the cops. It's not even that I wanted to protect Boss, because he was wrong for hurting Trish, but me and cops didn't get along. They locked my older brother up for fifteen years on a whack conspiracy charge. It tore my mother up inside, and she fell into a deep depression, leaving me to fend for myself. The police ruined my childhood, so I hated them. I would let a million murderers go free before I would help one cop. I knew Summer wouldn't understand it, but she would have to respect it.

She had stormed out of here before she gave me a chance to even explain myself. At first I was just going to let her stubborn self go, but I knew she needed me. She needed somebody. It was already apparent that her crew wouldn't be there for her from the way Mya tried to play her.

I eventually went after her, but I couldn't find her anywhere. She had a lot of options with fifty grand in her possession, so to look all over the city for her would be useless. She was probably hiding out somewhere, trying to figure out her next move.

I hoped that one of Boss's people didn't get to her. I would never forgive myself if anything happened to her. I knew she didn't have any other family, and I wanted to be her man so that she could at least depend on me. But she rushed out before I got a chance to explain to her how I felt.

I would have to keep my ear to the streets. I knew that everybody would be talking about her, and that Boss would definitely have Trish's funeral staked out with his goons, hoping to find Summer there in mourning. As if it weren't bad enough that Boss had murdered Trish, part of his setup was to arrange the funeral just so he could catch up with Summer. I hoped Summer was smart enough to stay away, but if I knew her like I think I did, then she would show up. She wouldn't be able to help herself.

I couldn't really blame her. It would be the last chance she got to say good-bye to the only family she had left. I knew that Trish and Summer had to be close. Before Summer came to town, Trish used to always brag about her baby sister. I couldn't see what all the hype was about. She didn't sound all that great, but when I finally met her, I understood. She was beautiful on the inside and hardened on the inside. I knew that wherever she came from, it hadn't been an easy journey, but I was feeling her harsh personality all the same.

I put my face in my hands as I tried to think of a place that Summer could have gone. *Where are you?* I thought, stressed out over her safety. I had to get to her first. Detroit was only so big, and Summer had people looking for her that she would never even suspect. Boss didn't need the $50,000. That little bit of money hadn't hurt his operation at all, but he was insane and got off on seeing other people suffer. If he felt like he had been disrespected, there were always consequences. If he caught Summer, he would make her pay for her sister's actions. He would make an example out of her, even though she wasn't the one who had stolen the money from him.

Summer against Boss was like David versus Goliath, only this time, I wasn't so sure that the good guy would win.

Chapter Nine

"Summer"

"I know who killed my sister," I announced as soon as Detective Myerss answered his cell phone.

"Excuse me? Who is this?" He asked. He cleared his throat and I knew that I had interrupted his sleep. It was late, but I didn't care. I needed his help—or better yet, I wanted to help him bring down Boss.

"This is Summer Flynt. My sister Trish was killed . . . you came and picked me up so that I could ID the body," I reminded him. "Do you remember me?"

"Oh yes, I'm sorry. I do remember you, Summer. I came by your place to take a statement from you, but your place was ransacked and you were nowhere in sight. I was hoping you'd contact me. I have a few questions for you. We think we have a couple sus-pects in your sister's case, but—"

"I know who killed my sister," I interrupted.

"Who?" The detective asked.

"A guy named Boss," I said.

"The boyfriend?" He asked skeptically. "The one who's making all the funeral arrangements?"

I was in true disbelief. How low could Boss go? Making the funeral arrangements for the person he murdered? I hadn't expected the police to know any-thing about Boss, but obviously they had done their homework. "If you know about him, why is he still on the street?" I asked.

"His story checked out and we couldn't find the murder weapon, so we were forced to switch our focus to other suspects," Detective Myerss answered.

"There are no other suspects. I'm telling you Boss did this!" I argued.

"Well, Ms. Flynt, without any evidence, that is merely just an opinion from a very hurt and scared little girl," he responded.

"What type of evidence do you need?" I ques-tioned.

"A smoking gun would be nice," he said smartly.

"What type of gun killed my sister?"

"A forty-five caliber handgun," he responded. "Now,

if you don't mind, it's late. If you have any other questions, please call me tomorrow."

"Yeah, sure," I said angrily. "By the way, when did Boss set the funeral date, and where is it being held?"

"In two days," the detective said. He put me on hold for a minute and then returned, giving me the name of the funeral home.

I slammed down the phone. I knew that I had just been brushed off. I was heated. Yeah, I was bitter, I was angry, and I was heartbroken over the death of my sister, but I was also right about Boss. If Detective Myerss wouldn't take my claims seriously, then I would just have to get the evidence against Boss myself.

Trish's funeral was in two days. The smart thing for me to do would be to steer clear. I knew that Boss and everybody else would be there just to see if I showed up, but how could I stay away? I had to pay Trish her final respects. There was no way I was going to miss seeing her one last time.

I decided to go to the funeral home a day early. I knew that Trish's body was already there and I figured that I could see her one last time in private. A wake was not being done for Trish, so no one knew that her body was prepared for viewing yet. I caught a cab to the home and put my hood over my head to conceal my identity at least a little as I got out of the car.

"How can I help you?" A woman greeted me.

"I'm here to see Trish Flynt," I said. My voice was low and emotional.

"I'm afraid you are a day early, young lady. The funeral isn't until tomorrow."

"Please," I begged. "She's my sister. I just want to say good-bye. Please." I knew that if the lady before me turned me away, then I would never see Trish again.

The lady sighed and then placed a gentle hand around my shoulders as she led me through two double doors. When I saw Trish's casket, the room seemed to shrink. I felt like I was suffocating, and all I could do to relieve my pain was allow the tears to run. I didn't make a scene or even allow a sob to escape through my lips, but my tears were pure, and I could not stop them.

I think the emotions I was feeling were too strong for my sixteen-year-old body to handle. I had never felt so empty inside; even when Mama died, I didn't feel this lost. Maybe it was because Mama was older or I was younger at the time, but whatever the difference was, I knew that my sister didn't deserve to by lying in this box at such a young age. She was only 21, and like so many other girls from the block, she had gotten caught up and was robbed of the rest of her time on this earth.

My rage and hatred for Boss only grew in those moments that I stood there, but I pushed my vengeful thoughts to the back of my mind and focused all of my energy on Trish. I wanted to remember everything. I wanted to be able to recall every feature on her face in her final moments. She was beautiful and so young. I knew that a part of me was leaving right along with her, and even though I didn't know anything about the afterlife, I hoped that there really was one. I wanted Trish to rest in peace, and I wanted to believe that my sister and mother were together again looking down on me . . . protecting me.

For so long, Trish had been like a mother to me. After Mama died, she stepped up and was there for me, even though we were both wards of the state. She made sure she taught me everything that our mother taught her. I wasn't robbed of any lesson that a mother would usually teach. Trish taught me how to keep myself up and how to carry myself like a young lady. She coached me through my first period and taught me how to stand up for myself . . . to never be afraid of anyone. She was probably the reason why I wasn't afraid to go toe to toe with a young man that most of the inner city feared.

I leaned down and kissed her on her cheek. "I love

you, sissy," I whispered. It took everything in me to turn around and start toward the door. These were my final moments with my only sister. I would miss her dearly, and no one could ever replace her.

In a way, I was jealous because she and Mama were together while I was all alone. I wiped the tears away and walked out.

Saying good-bye to Trish was one of the hardest thing I thought I would ever have to do. But something inside told me that things were about to get much harder.

Chapter Ten

"Summer"

"Summer . . ."

I jumped when I heard the male voice call my name as I stepped out of the funeral home. Jus stood before me, and he reached out his arm, signaling for me to step into his personal space.

"How did you find me?" I asked as I stared at his outstretched arm as if it were the plague. After our last encounter, I wanted nothing to do with him. He had clearly chosen sides and it wasn't mine.

"I'm not gon' lie, it took a while for me to figure out where you might go. At first I thought about catching up with you tomorrow at Trish's funeral, but I knew you wouldn't be dumb enough to go there. I also knew that you would never forgive yourself if you didn't say good-bye to your sister. I know how you think," he said as he wiped a lone tear off of my face.

I maneuvered away from his touch. I couldn't do this with him right now. My young heart couldn't handle any more pain.

"So what now?" I asked. "You work for Boss. What do you want from me?"

"I don't want anything from you. I just want to be with you, Summer. I know you're young and you are going through something right now, but I want you to let me in. I care about you," he admitted.

He pulled me close, and this time, I allowed him to hug me. His embrace was comforting and made me feel like I had someone to lean on.

"Let's get you out of here," he said as he looked around and pulled me over to his motorcycle. I grabbed his spare helmet and climbed on the back. I held on tightly and he pulled away.

I wasn't afraid even as he did 90 miles per hour through the city streets. There was nothing left to be scared of. At that point, I was simply living for one purpose—to destroy Boss. Everything else went out the window. All of the stupid things that I thought were important before seemed trivial now.

I felt Jus squeeze my hand while he steered the bike with his other hand. I held him tighter.

When we arrived at Jus's house, I hopped off the

bike and we rushed inside to avoid being seen by anyone.

"I'm glad I found you," he said when we were safely inside.

"Me too," I admitted as I kissed him. I don't know what made me do it, but I just wanted to have someone who cared about me.

He kissed me back, and our lip lock intensified until it was at a level that I was sure I couldn't handle. I wasn't ready for sex yet. I knew that I should stop and say no. I had heard the abstinence speech from many counselors, but it was so hard to resist when I was in the moment. And although my mind knew I was underage and was about to get into something that I wasn't ready to handle, my body urged me on.

I felt electricity in places where I hadn't even known there was an outlet, and before I knew it, I was in Jus's bedroom. I never said no; I won't even lie and say that I wanted to say no. I was all alone, and Jus made me feel needed. I felt wanted and loved, so I gave him something that I could never get back—my virginity.

It wasn't what I expected it to be. All the seductive songs about lovemaking and "Ooh yeah, baby, right there," I never got that. What I received was pain—excruciating pain—but I dealt with it because I thought it was what Jus wanted.

After it was over, I didn't regret my decision. I was lucky. I didn't get one of those stupid guys who would brag about me with all of his friends. Jus was a gentleman, and we talked all night. Our relationship had definitely changed.

"What now?" I asked.

"Now it's me and you against the world," he responded. "You shouldn't have made me wait so long."

That simple answer was like winning the lottery to me. I was vulnerable and I wouldn't say that he took advantage of that, but it made me want to be attached to him. If I had had a stable environment, I can't say that I would have been so quick to fall in love. It was young love, I'll admit, but love all the same.

"What about everything else?" I asked. It was like I wanted Jus to give me the answers to all of my problems. I wanted him to take control and handle what needed to be handled. Isn't that what he was supposed to do as my man, take charge and protect me?

Jus sighed. He looked me in my eyes and responded, "I want to be here for you. When I told you that I wasn't into snitching I meant that, but not because I was trying to protect Boss. I've had some bad experiences with cops, and I would rather not have anything to do with them. But I'll help you handle this."

"What bad experiences? If you don't mind me asking."

Jus told me about why he had beef with the cops. All I could say when he had finished telling me was, "Thank you, Jus. Thank you for helping me."

The fact that he was willing to put his personal issues to the side spoke volumes, and any reservations that I did have about being with him went out the window. When a person is my age, it's so easy for infatuation to transform into love, and for me, it had. I was in love with this boy. I knew that once this was over, we would be happy together. My entire world would be about him and his world about me. I would finally be able to find happiness. God had blessed me by bringing Jus into my life. I just couldn't believe that it had taken me so long to see it.

"I need to find the gun that Boss used to kill Trish," I said.

"Tomorrow we'll handle it."

I knew that the day of Trish's funeral was the best day to make my move. Boss and all of his goons would be at my sister's funeral, patiently waiting for my arrival. I may have been 16, but I had been around the block a few times and I was far from dumb. So while everyone who wanted my head sat through Trish's funeral, I would be at Boss's house, searching for the weapon that had he used to take a life.

Jus and I walked out of his apartment hand in hand. We were headed straight to Boss's place.

"You ready for this?" He asked to make sure that I could handle what I was walking into.

The situation had all of the ingredients for potential disaster, but I was doing it. I wouldn't be able to sleep at night if I didn't check Boss's arrogant behind and let him know that he wasn't as untouchable as he thought he was.

Jus popped his trunk and I climbed inside and curled up into a ball.

"Okay, here goes. I'll let you out as soon as the coast is clear," he promised.

I nodded and he closed the trunk gently. A few seconds later, I felt the car moving. The small space made me feel as if I couldn't breathe and I closed my eyes and imagined that I was somewhere else. I thought back to when it was just me, Mama, and Trish. Before I knew it, I almost forgot that I was hiding in the back of Jus's car. There was a smile on my face as I reminisced on all the good times we shared.

In no time at all, we arrived at our destination. I

had nervous flutters in my stomach and I took deep breaths to stay calm. I was truly banking on our plan to work, so I hoped everything went smoothly. If I had my way, Boss would be sitting behind bars by the end of the night.

Chapter Eleven

"Jus"

I got out of the car and tapped the trunk to let Summer know that I was going into Boss's house and she should stay quiet. The entire entourage was there. They were all dressed in street gear. It didn't matter that they were headed to a funeral. The young thugs wore what they wanted to wear. I spoke to a couple of people and then headed off to find Boss. I found him sitting inside his kitchen, laughing obnoxiously loud with one of his block lieutenants.

"Jus, what up, baby boy?" Boss greeted.

"You, fam. What's good?" I responded with my everyday demeanor.

I had worked underneath Boss for a long time, and for a moment I had a confliction of loyalty. Boss had put me on when I was too young to work anywhere else and had allowed me to make money to support my moms after she shut down from depression. I suddenly felt like a traitor. Yeah, Boss was cruel and unreasonable. He flooded the community with drugs and treated women like crap, but he had never disrespected *me* or done anything offensive to *me*. It was at that moment that I realized I had taken on Summer's beef.

I weighed my options in my head. I hated to send another brother to jail, but I loved Summer. I was feeling her more than I had ever felt any girl . . . ever. She was my girl, and for her and her alone I was going to go through with the setup.

"I can't wait to see the look on that li'l thief's face when I catch her. I'ma have people on every single door so that there will be nowhere for her to run. She's going to be all mine. I'm gonna show her what we do to thieves around here," Boss boasted.

"You know she really ain't the one who stole the money. You've already taken care of her sister. She's probably just running scared," I stated.

"I don't care who stole it. The point is she got it now. I'ma make an example out of her too. I'ma make sure don't nobody have the nerve to steal from me ever again," he seethed with rage.

"I feel that," I replied.

I had tried to calm Boss down, but after hearing his plans for Summer, he had become my enemy. I wouldn't let him hurt her. I couldn't.

"What about the block? Who gon' run the block while we're at the funeral?" I baited. I had to plant a seed in his head to make him think that someone needed to stay at his house to keep watch. I knew he didn't trust many people, so that someone would be me. Then once he was gone, I would let Summer out of the trunk and we'd search the place for the weapon.

"You're right, fam. That's why I like you, 'cause you're about your paper. You don't miss a dollar," he complimented. "You fall back and stay behind. We can handle the funeral."

I nodded and watched as Boss gathered up all of the henchmen and ushered them out of the house. He grabbed a set of keys off the table and gave me a pound before departing. As soon as the coast was clear, I could let Summer out and get the ball rolling.

Chapter Twelve

"Summer"

I panicked when I felt the car moving. *What is going on? This ain't part of the plan.* My heart began to beat out of my chest. I knew that something had gone wrong. The fact that the car was rolling and Jus wasn't the driver could prove deadly. If anybody besides Jus opened the trunk, then I was in trouble.

I had the cell phone that Tara had given me, and I struggled to pull it out of my pocket quietly. My hands shook uncontrollably as I fumbled to send a text message to Jus:

WTF? The car is moving, Jus. What happened? Where are you? Please help me. I don't know what to do.

I sent the text message and marked it urgent. Fear

began to creep into my heart as I waited for the reply that never came. It was the first time I realized exactly how dangerous my current situation was. I closed my eyes and prayed to God to help me out as I waited impatiently for Jus to come to my rescue.

Chapter Thirteen

"Jus"

When I received the text message from Summer that she needed my help, I didn't bother responding to it. I immediately rushed outside to find that my car was gone. It wasn't uncommon for Boss to take his workers' cars without giving them any type of notice. We were like a family. If he needed someone's ride, he just took it and would then hit them off with a couple hundred when he got back.

I punched the air and yelled, "No!" I couldn't believe I had slipped up like that. "How stupid could I be?" I asked myself. I couldn't believe that I had trapped Summer in the trunk and allowed the man who was looking for her to take the car. If something happened to her, it would be my fault.

I quickly dialed Boss's number to gauge his temperature. I needed to see if he had discovered Summer yet.

"What's up, fam? Everything's good?" Boss stated as soon as he picked up his cell phone.

"Yeah, I'm good on my end. I wanted to know how the funeral was going. I hate I'm missing all the action," I lied.

"We're just pulling up. You ain't missing anything. After I snatch this broad, I'm bringing her back to the house. She's gonna feel some pain. She won't be as lucky as her sister. I'm going to punish her slow," he stated.

"I think I'm losing service, fam. Call me when you get out," I stated before disconnecting the call.

Summer was in the trunk and may have heard everything that Boss had said. She had to be scared to death. That's when I realized that not only was she probably scared to death, she probably also thought that I had left her for dead. I quickly sent her a reply text:

He doesn't know you're in the trunk. Just stay calm and be quiet. Don't make any noise and just sit tight. If anything goes wrong, I want you to know that I love you, ma.

I wanted to keep her as calm as possible under the circumstances. On top of that, I wanted her to know that I had her back.

Chapter Fourteen

"Summer"

When the phone finally vibrated, alerting me that I had a text, I sighed a deep sigh of relief. I started to cry when I read Jus's response, not because he told me he loved me, but because he was preparing for the worst. I didn't want to die. How my plan had backfired and gone so horribly wrong I didn't know, but if I had to do it all over again, I knew that I would in an attempt to get justice for my sister.

I love you too, Jus.

I sent only those words back to Jus because there was nothing else to say. At this point, the only thing that I could do was wait until after the funeral was over. Hopefully I could go undetected until the car was returned to Jus. I would have to figure out another way to get into Boss's house, but at least I'd be alive to fight another day. Deep breaths helped to calm me down. I was lucky that it was cold outside or I would have roasted inside of the trunk.

I could hear Boss's voice. He was yelling instructions to his boys. The entire time I just tried to follow the instruction Jus had given me, which was to stay calm. That was easier said than done; nonetheless, I had done a pretty good job of it until the car slowed, then stopped, and I heard Boss give his boys a specific order:

"Yo, pop Jus's trunk to see if his spare pistol is underneath the spare tire," Boss ordered.

I almost peed my pants. I was caught, and there was nothing I could do about it. Seconds later, I heard the automatic lock pop. As soon as the trunk opened, I kicked whoever it was that stood over me.

"What the—!" The guy yelled in surprise as he stumbled back. Unfortunately my kick wasn't powerful enough to injure him. A twisted smile spread across his face when he realized what he had discovered. "Yo, Boss! Look who we have here," he reported.

Boss came around to the back of the trunk. He just looked at me and shook his head. "So it's like that, huh, Jus?" He said those words as if he were looking down at Jus and not me.

That's when his boy realized what my being in Jus's trunk meant. "This fool was hiding her in his trunk," he stated in disbelief. He actually had the nerve to laugh as he grabbed me roughly by the arm and shoved me back down in the trunk. "That's okay," he said, giving me the look of death. "Your little boyfriend can die with you."

I spit in his face and he smacked me hard, leaving my face stinging.

"Save it," Boss instructed as he walked back to the driver's seat. "Believe me; I'll let you have way more fun with her later."

His boy followed him back into the car after slamming the trunk closed. The car, once again, began to move.

I was scared and trembling. I no longer had the upper hand. I had heard Boss telling his boys how he planned on torturing me, and I was terrified. I tried to warn Jus that Boss knew what was up and that he was probably on his way back home, but the cell phone had no service in the area we were driving through.

"It was just working," I screamed in frustration as I put the phone back in my pocket. I had nothing left to lose. I began to bang on the trunk and scream in hopes of attracting anybody's attention. Now, the fact that it was cold outside played against me. At least in the summertime there was the chance of someone having their window down as they stopped next to us at a red light. Still, I continued to yell.

"Help me! Help!" I yelled over and over again as my fists pelted the metal above my head. I even kicked out one of the tail lights. I had seen that somewhere on a movie before. I didn't know how much good it would do, but I was willing to do anything to get out of that trunk. If I was lucky, a police officer would notice the missing light and pull Boss over.

"Please, help me!" I was screaming so loudly my throat was raw. I was desperate and shaking. I pulled out the phone and saw that I had one bar of service. I dialed 911.

"Nine-one-one. What is your emergency?" The operator asked.

"I've been kidnapped. My name is Summer Flynt. I need Detective Myers of the fifty-first precinct to come arrest Boss. He murdered my sister and now he's trying to kill me! Please!"

"Okay, Miss, just calm down."

"I can't calm down. Just shut up and listen. My name is Summer Flynt. I'm trapped in a trunk by a man who is trying to kill me. Send Detective Myers to Runyon Street on the East Side." I had given the location of Boss's house.

"Do you know the exact address?"

"No! Please help me!" I yelled. "Just get a hold of Detective Myers, please. He'll know what to do." I snapped the phone closed. I had to save whatever battery was left just in case I needed it again. I hoped and prayed the information I had given the operator was enough for her to send help my way.

As I felt the car come to a stop, I hurried to put the cell phone in my back pocket. I didn't want Boss to take it away. It was the only thing I had to call for help.

The trunk popped and then opened. Boss snatched me out of the trunk roughly, making me hit my head on the way out. Shoving me up the paved driveway, he didn't give me room to escape or even fight back. Besides, his boys had his back. I wouldn't have gotten too far.

Boss withdrew his gun and entered his house with me in a headlock.

"Jus, run!" I yelled when I looked up and saw him. It was too late. Boss had his gun aimed right at Jus.

Jus put his hands up. "Hold up for a minute, fam," Jus stated.

"Shut up and get in the basement," Boss yelled. Jus

hesitated. "Move now before I shoot your little girl-friend!"

His boys started to follow behind him, but then Boss stopped them. "Y'all go handle y'all's business in them streets," he told them. "I got this."

"You sure, Boss?" One asked.

"Positive," Boss replied. His boys did as they were instructed and left the house.

Jus walked down the steps, and Boss pushed me down the entire flight. We both backed up into a corner to create more distance between ourselves and Boss. He looked crazy as he pointed the gun our way.

"Chill out, Boss. She's got your money," Jus said, trying to negotiate our way out of trouble.

Boss chuckled softly, then smacked Jus with the butt of the gun. "Shut up! You going against the grain now? Huh, Jus?" Boss taunted Jus as he struck him twice more.

"No! Stop it!" I cried. Jus was on the floor with blood on his face. He was disoriented. "Jus, hold on!" I wished that I could take back the entire plan. Jus wasn't supposed to get hurt. Nothing was supposed to go down like this.

I reached into my back pocket and discreetly pressed the call button on the phone. I knew that it would redial the last number I had called. I only prayed that I had reception in the basement.

"Stop hitting him! This is between you and me!" I tried to keep a brave front up, but on the inside I was like Jell-O.

"Why did you kill my sister?" I asked Boss.

"She stole from me! I taught her a lesson just like I'm about to teach you," he threatened. He slapped me with the steel and I fell to the floor. "Your sister begged for her life. Let me hear you beg," he taunted.

The fact that he had the audacity to rub Trish's death in my face gave me strength that I didn't know I possessed. I kicked him directly between the legs, and he doubled over instantly. I didn't stop hitting him, though. I punched him repeatedly as he howled in pain. I ran to Jus's side and attempted to help him up so we could make a run for it, but as soon as we stood, we were knocked back down by Boss.

He pointed the gun at us, waving it back and forth between me and Jus.

"Wait! Just wait!" I pleaded. "Jus didn't have anything to do with any of this. Let him go. I'll stay. I snuck into his trunk," I lied. "He didn't even know I was there," I lied again, trying my hardest to sound and look convincing.

"Do I look stupid to you? He's soft. He's been soft on you since the beginning. Both of you are about to die, so you might as well say your good-byes," Boss said.

"You're going to kill me with the same gun you shot my sister with?" I asked.

"I wish I could use the same bullet, but the same gun will do," Boss stated.

He stood directly in front of me and pressed the gun to my head. I think he liked watching me squirm because he didn't pull the trigger instantly.

I closed my eyes, and my entire life flashed beneath my lids in slow motion. Everyone I loved had been taken by violence, and here I was preparing to leave this earth in the same exact way. My body shook uncontrollably and I tried to stop it. I didn't want to give Boss the satisfaction of knowing that I feared him.

I opened my eyes and forced myself to stare him in his face.

BOOM! BOOM!

"Freeze! Drop your weapon and put your hands in the air! Now!" The basement was flooded with police officers as they apprehended Boss and swept through his basement, checking everything to make sure it was secure.

I dropped to my knees and cried. I had never been so happy to hear the sound of the police in my life. *Thank God!* I had just been spared. I was within an inch of my life being taken away when the cops showed up.

Detective Myers strolled in with a radio in hand.

"Did you get all that?" a voice boomed through the walkie talkie.

"Copy that, I got it. We've found the girl . . . over," he responded. I pulled the cell phone out of my back pocket and tossed it to him.

"Thanks for coming," I said as I rushed to Jus's side.

"Thanks for calling," he replied.

The detective walked over to Boss and smiled smugly in his face. "It looks like I've got you confessing to a murder. The entire police force heard it, as a matter of fact."

Boss frowned and replied, "L-A-W-Y-E-R, pig."

"Not that it will matter. Johnny Cochran couldn't get you out of this one," the detective gloated.

I waited with Jus while a medic examined his nose to make sure it wasn't broken. He had a couple of cuts and bruises, but the bleeding made it look worse than it was. As the medics examined me, the cops started reading Boss his rights.

"Wait!" I called out to Detective Myerss before he could remove Boss from the house.

I walked over to Boss and stared at him for a few seconds. I hated his face. I hated everything about him. I poured all of my negativity and rage into him. I didn't want to carry it with me another day, so I transferred it into him and hoped that I had just made him as miserable as he had made me the day he took my sister's life.

I smiled and said, "Every morning when you wake up in your tiny cell, I want you to think of Trish. This is her revenge. I hope you rot in there."

I could tell my words got to him. His nostrils flared in rage, but I didn't care. I had gotten what I came for. Now it was over, and I could move on with my life.

Chapter Fifteen

"Summer"

After all the drama, I felt rejuvenated. It was like my life was finally on course and everything felt right. After Boss's arrest, I no longer had to hide. Nobody wanted to mess with me because I became known as the girl who beat Boss. My reputation preceded me, and everybody respected me on the block.

Detective Myerss discovered my real age, but because I had been so helpful in bringing down one of the city's worst criminals, he kept it to himself. I believe he knew my real age all along. Working for the system, he had enough resources right there at his fingertips to figure out anything he needed to know about me. I think he was just using his detective smarts by seeing what he could get out of me that would help in solving the case. Maybe if he had found that I was of no use, he would have turned me in. Maybe not. All I know is that Summer Flynt is still free.

I never told the detective about the money. I kept it because I felt like I deserved to. Fifty thousand dollars was my ace in the hole. That's a heck of a backup plan.

I moved into Jus's apartment and was prepared for my happily ever after. He was a good boyfriend. He was all that I had left, and I was happy that I had learned to trust him when I did. Jus was one of the good guys, but for so long I thought that he was just like everyone else. It was crazy how ironic it was that he and I ended up together.

I returned to school, but I only attended enough to keep my attendance records intact. I didn't want anyone coming around asking questions about why I had not been in classes and where I was. Until I was eighteen, I planned on being low key, so that I could continue to live on my own—which meant no rolling with cliques. I didn't need that kind of attention. I never wanted anybody to be in control of me again. Who needed parents or a guardian? Not me. I was young, smart, and had a stash full of money. I was more than capable of looking after myself.

I ran into Mya all the time, and she was as fake as ever. Once the contract was no longer on my head, she flipped the script and tried to play the role of concerned friend. I wasn't even buying the bull that she was trying to sell. When I needed her, she had not been there. She showed her true colors, and our friendship was worth nothing to her, so we could never be cool again. I kept my distance from her, even though all I really wanted to do was smack the taste out of her mouth. I kept it peaceful, though, on the strength of Tara. She was my one and only friend besides Jus, and I loved her to death. She was much more passive than Mya, and I didn't want to create tension between the two of them, so I didn't tell Mya about herself. I acted as if I didn't know how she had deceived me, but she knew something had changed. I barely even acknowledged her when we crossed paths. She was reduced from my girl to an associate that I hit with the head nod.

I really did not have a reason to dislike Latina. She and I were still social, but for some reason, I knew that if I had called on her for help, she wouldn't have been there for me either. But I hadn't actually called her, and I couldn't hold a grudge over something that had not actually happened, so she was still cool. She still had the biggest mouth in all of Detroit, but sometimes I used it to my advantage.

I made it a point to tell her about me and Jus, and just like clockwork, the news of the street's hottest new couple spread through the city like a wildfire. Latina was very good at what she did. Talking too much should be a profession, because she could start a rumor in no time.

Now the entire city knew that Jus was taken. A lot of chicks hated because he was a hot commodity. He was fine and all of the girls wanted him. I started to be hated by girls who were three years older than me. I guess they could not believe the fact that a sixteen-year-old had snagged Jus. Just like the entire world had done, those girls had underestimated me. They had counted me out of the race when in actuality, I was their biggest competition—the one to beat, for sure. I'm living proof that age really ain't nothing but a number.

My life was good for the first time since losing Mama. I didn't have anyone other than myself to worry about. I kept my nose clean and even started trying to convince Jus to get out of the streets. I tried to talk him into signing up for classes at the community college, but he was persistent in saying that school was not his thing. He told me that he didn't think that college was the only way for a young black man to be successful. I told him that I didn't think the streets were the only way for a young black man to be successful. He promised to weigh his options, and eventually find something that worked for him.

He ended signing up for barber school, which I thought was genius, because I planned on going to hair school as soon as I graduated. We made a plan to open up a his and hers salon, but as we all know, things don't always go the way they're planned.

Only time would tell what my future held, but right now, I was sixteen and the hottest chick on my block . . . and I was lovin' it!

I learned that it did not matter where I had come from. It didn't matter if I was the daughter of a doctor or a welfare mother. I determined my own future. I set the pace for my own life, and I was determined to make a better future for myself. I would make my moms and sister proud of me, because I knew that they were watching me from above, rooting for me to win. Legally I wasn't grown, but mentally I was wise beyond my years and blessed to have survived through the things that I had. Life couldn't be any better, and from this day forward, I was going to live it to the fullest.

Coming Soon . . .
May 2009

16½ On the Block

Prologue

I can't believe all of what I have gotten myself into this past summer. I'm sitting here looking at these four walls in this small room and wondering how I ended up in a girl's detention home. How in the world did I end up in the State of Michigan system?

Just a few months ago me and my Cass High School clique were riding in a drop top Lexus and singing Keyshia Cole's new song, having the time of our lives. But that all ended way too fast. As I look around this small room, all I can think about is how I would change what I did in the past if I could.

Oh, I forgot to introduce myself; I'm Latina Smith, the one and only. When I think about how my life changed so quickly in such a short time, I get dizzy.

As a matter of fact, the room feels like it's spinning out of control now. Everything seemed to happen all so fast.

When I stood in that courtroom and the judge sentenced me to three years of living in Detroit's detention home for girls, also known as DDHG, I almost fainted. He said I'm a menace to society and in desperate need of rehabilitation.

Whatever! I'm just a prisoner of circumstances. Any chick that has ever been in my shoes probably would have made pretty much the same choices. Yeah, there are one or two things I would have changed, but in most circumstances, my back was against the wall. My choices were limited if I even had a choice at all.

No one understands though, and no one ever will unless they know the entire story of deception, haters, my mistakes, my ups, and my downs. I want every young girl around the country to take heed to the life of Latina Smith, and in the end know that everything that goes up must come down. I didn't make it up; it's the law of nature.

Remember that everything that seems good isn't always good. I made the big mistake of letting something that seemed good mess up my life. Karma is real and I am living proof of that. And I feel as if I owe it to the next chick to keep it real and mine out there for them to live and learn. So sit back and pay close attention. I'm about to holla at y'all for a minute and let it be known how one weekend changed my life forever.

See, it all started on the last day of school, heading in the summer of 2009. I was 16, well 16 and a half . . .

Chapter One

"Me"

It was the last day of school of my tenth grade year at Cass High School and everyone was anxious about starting their summer break. Kids filed out of the doors as if they were animals as the zoo getting let out of a cage. I couldn't blame them though. I was just as amped as the next. I was now finally and officially a junior. Eleventh grade, here I come!

My girls and I where standing around and leaning against Asia's Lexus. Asia was the only one in school driving a 100,000 dollar car. Not even the teacher's could afford the spaceship that we were sitting on. It sat on 18 inch chrome wheels with Asia's name spelled on the license plate.

Asia was the daughter of a business man who

owned several pizza restaurants in Detroit and she was spoiled rotten, her and her half brother, who lived with them on the weekends only, but was usually out running the streets. Spoiled or not, that was my girl right there. She always wore the flyest gear and rocked the newest purses. She was the only chick I knew that had a real Gucci purse; not no fake knock-off folks buy at purse parties. And I knew a fake bag when I saw one. Heck, I used to get mine from the bootleg man right off of 7th Mile. Unlike me, though, Asia could afford the "real-deal".

Asia and I had been tight since elementary and were best friends. Last year, though, she didn't go to Cass. Her parents had forced her to go to a private school, so she and I hadn't hung as much last year as we had before. As a matter of fact, I rolled with another crew. But when Asia told me that she'd talked her parents into letting her attend Cass, I kicked those chicks to the curb. So this year it was just Asia and I and our other girl who we ended up hanging out with.

Our other girl's name was Gena. She was sooo ghetto, but I loved her. Even though she had the biggest mouth, she was the most petite out of all of us. She always kept long extension braids, because her mom had a beauty shop right off Grand River. Actually, now that I think about it, I've never seen

Gena's real hair. I wonder if she was bald-headed under that weave. Well anyways, even if her hair was fake, in life she always kept it real no matter what, and I loved her for that. I had met Gena in my freshmen year. She was in a couple of my classes. But by the end of our tenth year, all three of us were tight like hair weave glue.

As my girls and I bounced our heads to the music, we were checking out all the boys and trying to be seen as the sun gleamed down on the car and reflected off the red candy paint and chrome wheels. The sound of screeching tires erupted and everyone's focus went to the middle of the parking lot where Jus was burning rubber on his motorcycle.

Jus is what you would call a bad boy. It was known that he was in the streets and his parents let him do anything he wanted. He had graduated from Cass a couple years ago, but instead of seeking higher education in college, he seeked higher paper in the streets. And like the saying goes; seek and ye shall find, because he found it alright. Maybe that was why his parents let him do whatever, because he took care of his whole family. He pretty much made all the real money up in his house. Jus was what we called a "hood star". Jus hung out with a boy named Mike. Mike was fine as heck. He had long braids that hung down his back and a baby face, just like I liked it. I had a little secret crush on him, but I was always too scared to approach him.

"Jus is always trying to show off," Asia snapped as she blocked the sun from her eyes and flopped down into her seat. Just a second ago she had been standing up right outside her open car door with one foot propped up inside.

"Yeah, but he's cute," Gena said as she hoped in the backseat. I didn't see what she saw in Jus. He had some big ol' Jay-Z lips and his head was big. I would never talk to him. Besides, one of the girls in the clique I used to hang out with last year had already had him. Sloppy seconds sounded and looked gross in my eyes.

I got into the passenger side of the car and threw on my shades. "What are we doing tonight, ladies?" I asked as we pulled off.

"I think Mike throwing a party tonight at the hall on Woodward," Asia said as she maneuvered through the crowded parking lot. My heart fluttered at the sound of Mike's name, but you know I had to play it cool like I did not care.

"I don't know about that. I heard his parties get kind of crazy." I flipped down the visor mirror and checked my hair.

"Girl, please! Everybody knows that you got a mad

crush on Mike. Let's go, it might be fun," Asia said as she flipped down her shade.

"Heck yeah! You know you love you some Mike-Mike," Gena teased.

They were right, and I don't know who I thought I was fooling by acting like I wasn't diggin' on him. I did think Mike was kind of cute, but it wasn't anybody's business. That's why I chose not to speak on it. And I still wasn't ready to do so.

I didn't want to feed into what my girls were saying so I said, "Girl, I don't like Mike. Besides, every girl in school be all over him. I ain't got time to be creating enemies over that big head boy." I sounded so convincing I was about to start believing that lie my dang on self. "I'll go to the party though, but I have to ask my mom first," I added.

I skipped a couple songs on the mixed disk that was playing in Asia's system, turned up the music and closed my eyes, as I felt the wind blow through my hair. I loved the way it felt riding in a drop top on the high way. We all bounced crazy as the sounds of Soulja Boy's new song bumped.

After we dropped Gena off at her house, not too far from where I lived, my stop was next. Home sweet home . . . the projects. We pulled up into my apartment building and Asia turned up her nose as she always did. The sights of the crack heads walking around disgusted her I guess. To her it was the ghetto, but to me it was home.

I hopped out the car and yelled over the music, "See ya later! Call me in a couple of hours." I threw up the peace sign and flipped my book bag over my shoulder. I watched as Asia sped out of the apartment complex and then I focused on my building. Who was I kidding? Home or not, I hated it here.

It was so raggedy and old. Living in the housing projects was far from luxury and I couldn't wait until the day when I kissed that all good bye. I walked up the stairs that led to my place. Once in front of my door, I pulled out my key and unlocked the door. As soon as I opened the door I heard old-school music coming from the back bedroom. I knew my mother was home . . . and she had company.

The smell of a stinky, familiar odor invaded my nostrils and I knew what was going on in the back. My mother was doing drugs again. I became familiar with the smell of drugs at an early age, and although I hated what she did, that woman in the back bedroom was still my mother.

I had witness her downfall because of the drugs and I vowed to never let a drug enter my body. Not even weed. Although smoking weed was the popular thing to do amongst my peers, I decided not to fall into that lifestyle. I had more self-respect for myself than to fall victim to what many others before me had.

My mom had been battling a crack addiction for as long as I could remember. She spent most of the hours in her days out in the streets chasing that pipe dream. So I basically raised myself because of her absence. I am an only child so it has always been just me and my mom. Yep, me, my mom, and the pipe.

At first I went to my mother's bedroom door where the music was blaring from. I was going to knock and let her know that I was home, but I decided against it. I mean, why bother? Instead I went to my room to see exactly what I was going to wear to the party later that night.

I went through my closet and I didn't see anything fly enough fit to wear for the end of the year bash. On top of that, I didn't see anything fly enough for Mike to see me in. Unlike for Asia, money was tight in our neck of the woods. That meant I didn't have the biggest wardrobe, so I didn't have much too choose from in the first place. I was going to ask Asia if could I wear one of her outfits, but I didn't want anyone to notice that I was rocking my best friend's gear. That would totally ruin my reputation. But I knew I needed something to rock that night. I could not go up into Mike's party half-stepping. I wanted to be fresh just in case Mike saw me. I couldn't ask my mom for any money, because we were broke. It was the end of the month so I knew my mom's first of the month check was long gone. And if not, what ever money she might have had before I went to school that morning, was now a sticky, yellow substance. I was going to have to get it on my own, but there was one problem . . . I was dead broke.

I called Asia and asked her to take me to the mall so that I could get me something to wear to the party. Asia always loved an excuse to have to go shopping, so she was quick to be on her way. After she picked me up, I gave her directions to Oakland Mall, that was the. mall that all the people in my neighborhood shopped at. I had to get an outfit and still have time to go back home and get showered, dressed and do my hair and make-up, so going to a mall further out was out of the question for today. Besides, for what was about to go down, I needed to feel at home. I needed to stick to my neck of the woods where I didn't stand out.

When we pulled up to Oakland mall, Asia turned

up her nose and smacked her lips. "I don't know how you can shop at this ran down mall. It's so raggedy looking," she said as she whipped into a handicap parking spot.

"Well, Miss Big shot, everyone can't afford to shop at Somerset mall like you. Everyone doesn't have a rich father, feel me?" I said sarcastically as I opened the door to get out. "Let's go." Once I'd stepped out of the car I noticed that Asia wasn't moving. I bent down and looked inside only to see Asia sitting there with her arms crossed, planted in her seat like a stubborn, old mule.

"I'm not trying to get seen in this mall. I will wait outside for you. I don't want to mess up my rep," Asia answered. I didn't have time to beg her to come in with me, so I left her in the parking lot as I entered the mall. It was probably better that way anyhow. Little Miss Prissy probably would have stood out and drawn attention anyway.

Once I'd made my way into the mall, the first store I walked into was Macy's. As soon as I walked in I noticed a tall dark woman shopping and turned my butt right around and walked back out. See, Macy's think they're slick. They hire fake customers to walk around pretending to shop while all the while all they are really doing is keeping an eye on their real customers;

to see if anyone is going for the five finger discount. But Macy's wasn't fooling me. I knew every store's "pretend customer," and I wasn't trying to get caught stealing. I was too good to get caught anyway.

Since Macy's was a no go, I decided to go over to Fashion's Inc. Now that joint was the hardest store to steal from because they had cameras up around every corner of the store. But the outfit I needed for tonight was crucial, so I would just have to take my chances there. I had to get fly for later that night. And with no cash to my name, I was left with no choice but to engage in every store manager's nightmare; the five-finger discount.

Stealing is a bad habit I picked up from my mother while I was growing up. In between the first of the month's checks, my mother boosted clothes from stores and sold them half off the ticket price to people in the neighborhood. I started honing in on the craft of boosting quite young thanks to my mother. And not just because she took me with her on her small heists, but because she used me as part of her scheme.

My mom had me putting cloths in my book bag at the age of eight years old. She would make me think we were playing a game called, "Don't let the security guard see." I used to have so much fun playing that game at the stores. Mom and I were like the Pink Panther minus the theme music creeping up and down the aisles.

I remember one time Mom and I were boosting in a store and she had just stuffed a black, velour jogging suit down my book bag when a female store clerk approached us.

"Excuse me, Miss," the clerk had said.

Mom and I nearly jumped out of our skin. I swear her hear and mine were doing a collabo on beats.

Mom put on the best sweet and innocent face she could muster up and replied, "Yes?"

"The store is having a special today." The woman handed Mom a flyer. "If you open up a store credit account with us, you'll get twenty percent off your first purchase. That's five percent more than usual."

"Oh, wow." Mom feigned excitement as she looked down at the flyer. "I think I just might take you guys up on your offer today. I mean, heck, my money is running so low, every little discount would help."

And boy was mom right. Every little discount would help, but as the lady walked off and we walked out of the store, the 100% off discount turned out to be far more appealing than the one the clerk had to offer.

In all honesty, I have to admit that those boosting

days with my mom were the best. I think during that time, it was the only memories I have of my mother and I doing something together. But now things have changed. She's all about herself, and me, Latina Smith . . . I'm all about me!

Chapter Two

"Mike"

Life wasn't easy for ya' boy. I had two little brothers and one little sister, all under the age of ten. I was the oldest at 16 and we all lived with my 67 year-old grandmother whom we called Big mama. We all lived in a three bedroom house and it was so cluttered, one could hardly think straight up in that piece.

My grandmother had been taking care of us since I was ten years old when my mother suffered from cancer and died two days before my tenth birthday. Like some of the other kids I grew up around, I never knew my father. Everything had been going good with Big Mama thought, that was until I just recently learned that the wonderful state of Michigan was going to cut off my grandmother's aide for us within the next six months.

I can't help but wonder how the government could be so cold? How did they expect my grandmother to be able to feed us and keep a roof over our heads without the assistance she'd been counting on to help her raise us?

I knew we had to figure out a way to bring more income into the place. Of course, I was the only one of us kids who was old enough to work. I thought about going to sell drugs and try to help Big Mama out, but I couldn't run the risk of getting caught and leaving my sibling and Big Mama to fend for themselves. So, I landed me a gig at the boxing gym that was around the corner from our house instead. Although it wasn't that far, Big Mama let me use her car to get back and forth. She said she didn't want me walking home in the dark. Besides, she never really drove it anyway. Everybody just assumed it was my car.

At the gym I swept the floors and cleaned up the place three times a week for Mr. Johnson, a former golden gloves champion for Detroit. He was a good guy. He even gave me his old–school Cutlass to drive since I didn't have a car; one of the perks of the low paying job. But I ain't complaining. Every little bit helped.

Another perk was the use of one of Mr. Johnson's

other facilities that sometimes doubled as a gym and a hall. On occasion he'd rent out the facility to personal trainers or boxers who wanted to be trained in private. He'd even rented it out to churches before to hold Bingo. Mr. Johnson decided to let me rent it out at a discount to throw a big end of the school year party in the hall, that wasn't too far from where the boxing gym was located. I was going to charge fiver dollars a person to get into my party. Hopefully, I would make enough that night to help Big Mama with her mortgage this month.

I watched as my little brothers and sister came in from school. I had already made them up some peanut butter and jelly sandwiches to eat for their after school snack. It seemed like I had been preparing meals more and more, since Big Mama's arthritis stopped her from moving around a lot.

"Sup, Mike-Mike?" My little sister said as she sat her book bag down and hopped in the chair. She was the only girl and the youngest at seven years old.

"Hey, big head. Go wash your hands before you eat," I said as I finished putting the paper plates on the table for my other two brothers, Jake and Blake. They were nine year old twins . . . bad twins. The doctor's said they suffered from Attention Deficit Disorder (ADD), but I think they were just very energetic. It seemed like they moved 100 miles per hour all the time. I never saw any humans so hyper. They never seemed to slow down. They ran in and immediately began to pound on the table, trying to do the freshest hip hop beat they could do.

"Calm down, fellas," I said as I cracked a smile and put their sandwiches on their plates. "Go wash ya hands before you eat." That's when Angel, my little sister, came from the bathroom and had her hands on her hip.

"Mike-Mike. The water doesn't work anymore," she complained with a frown on her face, not understanding that the water was turned off. I took a deep breath and went over to the kitchen sink and turned on the faucet. Nothing came out and I knew that the city had finally got fed up with all of Big Mama's failed promises to pay and had turned the water off. We had been behind on our payments for three months now and it caught up with us. I didn't know what to tell them. I didn't want to let them know we were struggling. I didn't want that on their young minds, so I lied.

"The water bandit came and stole all of the water," I told them with a big smile spread across my face. The kids started laughing and I was relieved that they'd fallen for it again. It was just a couple months ago when right in the middle of our watching a *Different Strokes* rerun that the television went out.

At first I'd told them that something was wrong with the electric circuit or something; that there was a problem with the fuse box. But then they started demanding that I fix it, even though I knew darn well that that wasn't where the true problem lied. The three of them had this look on their faces, urging me to go hurry up and make everything alright. After all, that's what they expected of their big brother, to make everything alright. I couldn't let them down. So after pretending to mess around with the fuse box in the basement, I came back upstairs and gave them the story about the electricity bandit.

I compared the electricity bandit to that of a tooth fairy who runs around stealing teeth. But then I got stumped when Angel explained to me that the tooth fairy wasn't really a bandit, because at least she left something for what she had taken. Of course after that she asked me what it was the electric bandit had left for us.

"Candles," Big Mama had saved the day with her words when she came walking out of her bedroom and downstairs to the living room where we all sat..

"Candles?" my three siblings asked, giving each other puzzled looks.

"What we gon' do with some candles when we ain't even allowed to play with matches?" Angel asked, never the one to leave well enough alone.

"This is what you do." Big Mama walked into the kitchen and pulled out a few candles from a kitchen drawer.

It was only six o'clock in the evening, but the clocks had been moved forward an hour, so it was getting dark outside. Big Mama retrieved a glass candle holder for each of the candles from a cabinet. She then walked over to the stove and turned it on. Thank goodness we had a gas stove and she was able to light the candles.

After Big Mama lit the candles, she placed them on the living room table. We all sat around the table while Big Mama led us in some songs she said she used to sing with our mother when she was a little girl. Songs like "There's a Hole in My Bucket," "Mary Mack," and "Found a Peanut." But it was Big Mama teaching us how to sing "Row Your Boat," in sequence that was most fun. I have to admit for something that could have turned out to be a depressing and frustrating time, Big Mama turned into one of the most memorable times ever.

And because of Big Mama backing me up about the electricity bandit, today, it made the story about the water bandit all the more believable.

"Now get at the table and eat," I ordered my siblings, "so that you guys can start your homework."

I left them at the table and went upstairs where Big

Mama room was. Just as I expected, she was lying in her bed, in her room, watching her judge shows. Big Mama loved her some Judge Mathis.

"Hey, Big Mama," I said as I stuck my head in her room.

"Hey, baby. How was school today?" She answered in her raspy voice.

"It was okay. They came and turned off the water today," I said without enthusiasm.

"I know . . . I know. Baby." Big Mama struggled a little to sit up I her bed. "Come over here and sit down fa' a minute," she said as she patted her bed. I walked over and took a seat right next to her as she continued. "Times are hard right now. They taking away my checks and it's getting too much to take care of all of you. I have been praying every night and I know somehow, someway we're going to be alright. I just need some help, ya know," she said. Big Mama never really showed weakness and that was my first time hearing her talking as if she couldn't make everything aright. The same way my younger brothers and sisters expected me to always make things alright, I expected the same out of Big Mama. But now it seemed as though I would have to step up big time.

"Big Mama, don't worry about anything. I am going to get some money and make sure we are going to be okay." I looked at Big Mama with confidence and put on a fake smile. I knew she was hurting on the inside and I had to do something about it.

It was six o'clock in the evening on Friday night and I only had a couple hours until my party started. It was my goal to set it off proper like, and with the help of my boy, Jus, I had no doubts that it was going to be one of the most talked about parties since the ones this street cat named Boss used to throw. As a matter of fact, before Flint's finest threw Boss in jail, Jus used to be one of his homeboys. Now it was Jus and I who were tight like the fist on the afro picks.

Jus and I had known each other since we were young, and we'd always been pretty tight. It's just that for a minute there he was extra tight with Boss. But now that Boss was out of the picture, Jus and I were tight again like the old days.

Jus was the type of dude who lived for the day. He had a crazy personality and a free spirit. He rode his motorcycle like a madman and lived life on the edge. He dealt drugs and always tried to get me to join him in his illegal hustle. But like I said before, I didn't feel it was worth it. if I ever got caught. It wasn't just about me. My being incarcerated would be affecting other people's lives around me. My sibling needed me. Big

Mama needed me, and I was going to make sure that I was always there for them.

Jus and I were sitting on my porch talking about the party that was about to go down in a couple of hours. We were just double checking with each other to make sure everything was on point.

"Tonight it is going to be popping. All the ladies are going to be all over me, watch!" Jus yelled as he rubbed his hand over his braids. I laughed at Jus' arrogance and began to stare at the ground. I was lost in my own thoughts about how I would come up with the cash for the water to be turned back on.

"So how much do you make grinding?" I asked my dude, just out of curiosity, of course.

"Man, I get that paper, homey," he said as he pulled out a wad of money.

My eyes lit up when I saw him with all that money.

"How much?"

"It all depends. Sometimes I make more in one day than a whole month's work. But sometimes it's slow," Jus said as he began to keep it real and lost the macho attitude. That's when he pulled out a gun and showed it to me, trying to show off.

"Yo, is that real?" I asked as I stared at the iron.

"Yeah, it's real." Jus must have noticed the way I was admiring the gun, that my hands were a virgin to a cold piece of steel such as that. He pushed the gun towards me. "Here . . . you can hold it."

Jus handed the gun over to me. I examined it carefully and picked it up and pointed it in the air. It was my first time ever touching a gun.

"You know what? You can hold that for a minute. I have another one," Jus said as he grinned.

"What do you mean? I don't need a gun," I was quick to say as I tried to hand it back to him. If Big Mama ever got wind of me having a gun, let alone bringing one into her house, the next thing to go out would be my lights; because Big Mama sure wouldn't have no problem in knocking them out.

"No, you just hold it for me," Jus insisted as he put his hand up, denying the gun.

Just then I heard the front door creek open behind me and knew it was either Big Mama or one of my siblings. So I quickly put the gun in my hoody to get it out of sight. I wish I would have known at that point, but it would be later when I realized that was the biggest mistake I'd ever made in my entire life . . . and it wouldn't be the last.

Chapter Three

"Me"

"Hey, stop!" the guard yelled as he chased me trough the JC penny's parking lot.

I had a bag full of clothes in my book bag as I ran for dear life. I tried to run as fast as I could to get away from his fat butt, but he was right on my tail. Had he eaten one more donut for breakfast that morning, I think I could have gotten much better of a lead on him. But it appeared as though the lead I had on him was plenty.

I quickly jumped into Asia's car. "Drive! Drive!" I ordered her, half out of breath.

Without verbally asking all the questions that were written all over her face, Asia was quick, fast and in a hurry to speed off, leaving the guard in the dust after almost running over him when he tried to play superman and stop the car by standing in front of it and pressing down on the hood.

"Girl, what happened?" Asia finally asked as she drove out of the mall's parking lot, frequently checking her rear view mirror to make sure that we weren't being followed.

"His fat butt was following me around the store," I replied to Asia, breathing heavily. "I think he saw me on the cameras all along stealing. So when I was about to leave, he began to try to get close. So I said 'forget it' and took off running." I hoped she'd hold off on the questions for a minute as I still struggled to catch my breath.

Although my initial intentions when going to the mall was just to get a fly outfit for the party tonight, I had a bad habit of getting greedy and sometimes picking up more than I was supposed to when I went to the mall.

That wasn't the first time that I used my five finger discount to get some clothes, and Asia was well aware of my little addiction. So my story as to why the security guard was chasing me was no surprise to her.

I was finally able to catch my breath, and after getting myself together, I pulled out the clothes from my book bag. I held up the Baby Phat shirt I had nabbed and examined it.

"That's cute, girl," Asia complimented after she glanced over at the pink shirt.

"Yeah I know. That's why I got it," I said sarcastically.

I had managed to stuff two whole outfits into my book bag and now I was ready to hit the party. Asia wanted to stop by her house so that I could help her pick out her outfit for the party. I loved going to Asia's house. It always reminded me of what I wished I had. They lived in a mini mansion in Auburn Hills, a suburb just outside of Detroit.

When we pulled into her driveway, this time like all the other times, I stared at the two story brick house in awe, daydreaming about me living in something so spectacular some day. But how we'd ever afford it was beyond me. Heck, I wish I even just knew my father, let alone have one such as Asia's that owned a successful pizza chain.

We entered the house and the white carpet seemed like it was brand new. It nearly blinded me it was so bright white. I followed Asia into her room and sat on her bed while she began to search through her closet, which was like a small boutique in itself. Girls like her never had to worry about not having something to wear and how to get it. I guess some people were just more blessed than other. I wasn't hating on my girl or anything. That was just life. She couldn't help it if her father was about something and mine wasn't crap.

"What do you think about this?" Asia asked as she held a black Dior dress up to her body. Honestly, I thought the dress was whack, but I didn't want to offend my girl so I lied. And plus, I didn't want her to look better than me, so it wouldn't hurt any for her to wear that ol' ugly dress.

"Girl, that is too cute," I lied.

"Tina! I know when you're lying!" Asia said with a skeptical look on her face.

I had to admit it, my girl knew me too well.

"Okay, okay. That is hideous. Try something else," I admitted with a chuckle that stated, "I'm busted."

Asia began to look through her closet, and we went through at least fifteen outfits and Asia still wasn't satisfied with one. She finally gave up and closed her closet.

"I'm just going to have to go to the mall and pick out something special for the party like you did. I need to be rocking something new and fly anyway," Asia said as she headed out of her bedroom and down to her living room. I was close on her heels.

"Why didn't you tell me while I was at JCPenny's? I would have gotten you something and only charged you half the price," I said, wishing she would have said something earlier. That extra change in my pocket would have done me good.

"I do not wear clothes from JCPenny. No offence or anything, but I just don't get down with that store." A disgusting look washed across Asia's face. She reminded me of Hillary from *The Fresh Prince of Bellaire*. "Just think about it," Asia added arrogantly.

She always acted like she was above everyone, but that was just her personality, and she was my girl, so I tolerated it.

Asia exited the room and I followed her as she made her way to the big painting that hung over their fireplace. She began to reach for it and I was wondering what in the world she was she doing. How did she go from being desperate about finding an outfit to wear to the party tonight, to admiring art?

"What are you doing?" I asked.

"I'm hitting the stash." She took the picture down, revealing a small steel safe that was built into the wall where the picture once hung.

"Hitting the stash?" I asked, not knowing what she was talking about.

"Yeah. Anytime I need a little extra cash, I just take a little." She said it so nonchalant as if every girl our age had a safe full of money they could just go hit up whenever they need some cash.

"Aren't you worried that your father will catch you?" I asked.

Asia proceeded to open the safe, exposing the piles of money inside. I almost choked when I saw how much was in there. Just five minutes ago, I'd almost gone to jail for trying to steal a couple outfits, and this girl had access to enough money to dress every body at the party. But I wasn't tripping.

"He doesn't even count this. He brings the money from the restaurants in here every night and just dumps it in here."

"But how do you know that he doesn't count it at the restaurant before he brings it home?" I asked.

Asia sounded so sure of herself when she replied to my inquiry. "He only counts it when he takes it to the bank Saturday morning." Asia was telling all of her father's business. And people used to accuse me of having a big mouth and telling everything. Asia had me beat, and that is exactly why I never told Asia anything. She couldn't hold water and she would let everyone in Detroit know your business.

As Asia did what she had to do, I went and sat down on the sofa. After Asia took a couple hundred dollars or so, we left out for the mall. This time we went to the one that was around the corner from her house. The clock was ticking and we didn't have much time at all before the party started. So, we really needed to put a move on it because I was really looking forward to partying . . . Naw, I'm lying. I was looking forward to seeing Mike.

The party was jumping and the hall was packed. All of Cass High School was there celebrating the end of the school year and the beginning of our summer vacation. You couldn't even tell that the place was a boxing gym. It looked so different. Everyone was going crazy to the Souljah Boy's song that was blaring through the speakers. They were all doing the dance that went along with the song while I just sat back and watched.

It was dark in the hall and the only shine was from the strobe lights. I was standing against the wall with my girls and looking at the people dance on the dance floor. That's when I noticed Mike across the room standing on the opposite wall. He was surrounded by his boys and seemed like he was looking our way. So I tried to look as good as possible and pretend like I didn't notice him. But how could I not? He was fine. He had neat braids that were so long and thick, and he had a muscular build that I loved. He was by far the finest boy in school. I felt Gena nudge me to try to get my attention.

"You see Mike over there staring at you?" Gena asked as she sipped her bottled water.

"He's not looking at me," I said as I quickly glanced over there.

"I don't know. It sure looks like he is staring your way to me," Asia just had to add in her two cents. "I'm about to go ask him," she said.

Before I realized what Asia had just said, she was heading over towards Mike and his boys. I turned as red as an apple out of humiliation. Asia always did crazy stuff like that.

One time when we were all at the mall, and there was this dude who worked in the Foot Locker store that kept eyeballing Gena. Unfortunately, he wasn't the most appetizing fry in the combo meal, so Gena tried her best to ignore him. Everytime Asia and I would nudge her shoulder and inform her that he was still staring her down, she'd get mad. She finally told us that if the boy looked a little better, she'd at least go out with him just so she could use his employee discount and buy her some shoes. Well, the next thing we knew, Gena and I looked up to see Asia over there talking to the guy, while pointing at Gena. A few seconds later, Asia came waltzing back informing Gena that the guy would be glad to let Gena use his employee discount if she went out with him. It was a mess. The three of us never laughed so hard in our lives. But the very next week, we each got a pair of shoes for almost half off. And Gena got a free meal at O'Charley's.

I had to admit though, even though I now knew first hand what Gena must have felt like as I stood here embarrassed watching Asia go over there and start talking to Mike, I almost hoped I'd be sharing a meal at O'Charley's with Mike.

I casually looked across the room to see if Asia was really going to talk to him. I glanced over there and saw her talking to him. I couldn't believe her! Asia came back with a big smile on her face. I was ready to curse her out, but she spoke before I could get my words out.

"Mike wants to talk to you after the party. He said to meet him on the rooftop afterwards."

I wanted to be mad because Asia went over there and talked to him on my behalf. I didn't want Mike to think I was some punk, or that I was too stuck up to come over there and talk to him myself that I had to have my girl do the dirty work. But I couldn't help but to smile at the result of Asia's efforts. That was the best news of the day. I have wanted to talk to Mike since freshmen year.

"Asia, what did you say to that boy?" I asked as she stood next to me.

"I told him that he needed to stop fronting and

come over here and talk to you," she said with a big cheesy smile. I playfully punched her in the arm and told her she was wrong, but on the inside, I was glad she stepped to him for me, because no matter how bold I sometimes believe myself to be, I probably would have never done it myself.

"The party was jumping tonight. What a way to start off our summer," Gena said as we made our way to the parking lot.

"Yeah, it was nice," Asia added.

I saw Mike standing right outside of the door once we made our way out. He was surrounded by his friends as he thanked some of his guests on their way out for coming to his party. I don't know how I managed to forget that I was supposed to meet Mike on the rooftop, but I was steady heading to the car right along with my girls.

"Are you going to meet Mike on the roof or what?" Asia asked as we approached her car.

"Oh, yeah. That's right," I remembered.

"Girl, stop playing," Asia stated. "You know you been waiting all night to get with that boy."

"No, for real, I forgot," I told her.

"Yeah, right." She shooed her hand at me like I was

a fly. "Anyway, don't be too long. We'll wait for you in the car."

"Oh, that's okay. Y'all don't have to wait for me. I will see if Mike can just take me home," I told Asia. That's when I saw Jus and his friend walking toward us. Then there was the sound of police sirens and flashing cop lights. A swarm of patrol cars sped down the street right pass us.

"I wonder who they are after. I wouldn't want to be them," Jus said as he approached us. He threw his arm around Gena, trying to run game. They began to have a personal conversation.

"Are you sure you don't want us to wait?" Asia asked as she hopped on the hood of her car, trying to look cute. "Looks like we gon' be out here a minute anyway." She nodded towards Gena who was all smiles up in Jus's face.

"Yeah, I can handle myself," I assured her. "I will call you when I make it home."

"Okay, girl. Have fun." She said devilishly. "But not too much, if you know what I mean."

"See ya, Tina," Gena added as she finished up her conversation with Jus and went and got in the car.

"See y'all chicks later" I said just before I turned around to see where Mike was at.

I spotted him still standing by the door talking to

Mr. Johnson, the man that owned the place. He just happened to look up while I was standing there gazing at him. I quickly turned my head away so that he didn't think I had been stalking him or nothing like that.

I folded my arms and tapped my foot. I spoke to a couple of people I knew from Cass and then turned my attention back to where Mike had been standing. I saw him by the building's door, and once again, he saw me. We locked eyes and then I followed his as he looked up towards the rooftop and then back at me. Next he entered the building and I knew that was my cue.

I smiled and followed him inside, knowing that he wanted me to come and meet him at that moment. I made my way back inside the door and then followed an exit door and a flight of steps up to the rooftop. When I made it to the top, I saw Mike standing there smiling as he stared at me.

"What up, Tina?" he said.

"What's up, Mike?"

"Nothing much. Did you enjoy the party?" He asked.

"Yeah, you fixed up Mr. Johnson's place pretty nice. It seemed much bigger tonight for some reason."

"Yeah, Mr. Johnson was cool for letting me throw

my party here. It's going to take weeks for me to work off the debt. One of my perks for working for him is that I got a discount. But you know how cheap he is. It wasn't much of a discount," he said right before we burst into laughter.

"You. I wanted to holla at you. You know I'm feeling you, right?" He said as he released his charming smile.

I began to blush, not knowing what to say. Then I realized that what better thing to say than the truth. Heck, I was feeling him too and I needed him to know. Him knowing how I felt about him could make for a much better summer than playing cat and mouse and all summer long.

Before I could open my mouth to answer him, I heard two men yelling at each other from afar. Both me and Mike's eyes shot to the building next door, where we saw two men with ski-mask on the roof arguing about something. The buildings were very close . . . only about two and half feet apart, so we had a pretty clear view.

One man was slim and tall and the other one was short and fat. The men didn't see us; they were too busy cursing one another out. Both men had guns in their hand, and when I saw that, I immediately ducked behind the chimney. Mike followed my lead and ducked behind it also.

"What's going on?" I whispered as I peeked around the chimney and stared at the two men. One of the men had a duffle bag in his hand as the other man tried to take it from him.

Mike stood up some and peeked over top of my head. "I don't know. Seems like they're arguing over that bag." Mike stuck his head out a little more trying to get a better look. We both remained silent, almost to the point where we didn't even breath, in order to listen better to that we could try to hear exactly what was going on.

"Forget that! I'm keeping the money! I don't trust you," the taller man said as he gripped the bag.

"No, I'm keeping the dough!" The other insisted as he reached out for it. The other man jerked it away before his partner could get a good grip.

"Let's just hide it here until the morning and come back for it. It's too hot for either of us to keep it on us for now."

The men looked around and Mike and I ducked down, trying not to be seen. The man with the bag went over to the other building's chimney and stuffed the money in one of its vents. "We will keep it here and come back for it in the morning."

The shorter man didn't sound like he was down with that as his voice was laced with doubt when he stated, "Naw, man, I don't know about that. Just give me my little cut right here and just go on about our night. You feel me?"

"Are you dumb? It's too hot right now. The police are all over the place. We need to dump it here."

"I guess that's cool. But don't try any funny stuff. We will meet back up here tomorrow first thing."

"Okay," the man said as they both took off their mask and tossed them over to our building. They landed right by us. My heart began beating fast. I was scared that the men would see us hiding, but I guess they didn't because they exited the roof.

Once the men were gone, Mike and I both took deep breaths before we came out of our hiding spots.

"Did you see that?" Mike asked as he slowly rose up.

"Yeah. This is some crazy stuff" I answered.

Silence wrestled between us momentarily as we each looked over at the other building's chimney.

"We should go and see how much is over there," Mike said. "It's not that far of a jump." He examined the distance. "Two feet, three feet tops of a jump from here to there."

I visually measured the distance myself, and Mike was right, it didn't seem to far of a jump. I then looked up at Mike and that's when I saw that infamous look of greed in his eyes. It was a trait of every ghetto child, no matter who they daddy was. We all inherited those eyes.

For a minute, I was skeptical about getting involved, but that duffle bag seemed full, and I was in desperate need of money. Another trait of the ghetto child.

I thought for a moment before reply, "Let's wait a few minutes just to make sure they're gone first, and then we'll go over," I said.

The look on Mike's face was unforgettable. He looked at me like I was the Bonnie to his Clyde. He nodded his head in agreement, and after a couple minutes, we headed over.